GOD LOVES BLACKWOMEN WHILE NIGGAS LOVE BITCHES!

PaPa Sak

INTRODUCTION

This book is dedicated to many people. It would be difficult to name everyone but I must admit that stories come from people in your life past and present. Extraordinary people whose lives must be told inspired this novel. I am by no means an expert on male/female relationships. I have had my failures and I have had my successes in the arena of love. My objective is to tell good stories with the intent to inspire, consider, and enlighten. I truly believe that should be the goal of an Agriot (Storyteller) or Tajedi. With that in mind I dedicate this book to family, friends, foes, acquaintances and mostly to God. Whether you call him Allah, Yahweh, Jehovah, Jah or just simply God he is the root to everything we do for the upliftment of humanity.

We as Black people are in a serious condition. We have lost the value of family and have replaced it with the value of things. Our relationships do not have the staying power of the past. Marriages fall apart because of some of the most trivial things. We make love a complicated thing. The truth of the matter is that since our families have fallen apart we as a people grow farther and farther apart. At one time family was the basis of the community. Black people that live next door to one another today hardly speak to each other. This is a travesty and the blame goes to the principles we live by.

Since our sojourn in North America our families have been broken up by design. The intent was to never have our families united and strong because strong families made strong communities. Strong communities in turn created strong power bases. But since a permanent underclass is necessary to sustain a capitalist society we were encouraged to fail at building strong families. The individual was the only concern and the community took a back seat.

The science of how to mate was never taught to us. The yardstick that determined a good man was never implemented. The yardstick that determined a good woman was never implemented. So millions of Black people come up every day with different ideas of what is a good man or good woman. We have grown to worship the attainment of money, sex and power. I'm not suggesting these are bad things to attain but not to the point where we have lost the value of true love. In the scriptures it says that 'God is Love' which suggests that love is the most creative force in the universe. When you truly 'fall in love' you are being creative on higher levels than just sex. But sex and money has determined the yardstick of what is good and what is not good. So our search to fulfill our lustful desires has devoured our desire to find true love. In these failed relationships children are produced and the cycle continues.

If we were to redirect our energy to finding compatible principles in a mate we could probably start having stronger families. Basic principles would be commitment, respect, obligation, responsibility, compatibility, honesty and faith as a foundation. Then we could choose mates that have similar objectives because we look for those principles first. Many women claim they are looking for good men but search in a cesspool full of men that think with their private parts. Instead of considering the thoughts and actions of a man they chase after the men that can't grasp the concept of knowing how to love. Men say that there are mostly no good bitches and hoes in the world today but they search in a cesspool full of women that think what is between their legs and the shapes of their bodies is their most valuable asset. We as men see physical beauty and allow our lower desires to dictate how to properly choose a woman. We all have a lot of growing up to do. We are grown children playing with dangerous weaponry. If we all learn to love properly we can build stronger families. That is the premise of this book.

Lastly this book is dedicated to my family. I also would like to thank all my supporters of the Etched N Stone Company for their commitment to excellent book making. I also would like to thank Tatiani Ambrose Mercer and Chris Barfield for posing for the original cover of my book. Two beautiful young people that I am glad are in my life. I also would like to thank Je'licia Hardison for agreeing to do this photo shoot and being on the new cover of this book. Last but definitely not least are the fans that supported my last book, my first book, 'The Wages of Sin' A gangster's story. I hope you enjoy.

Sincerely
PaPa Sak
The Kingpin of the Ink pen

Self-analysis is the key to healthy relationships between Black men and women!

GOD LOVES BLACKWOMEN WHILE NIGGAS LOVE BITCHES
TABLE OF CONTENTS

On the edges of panic my turmoil is unseen
Viciously eating away my spiritual protein
I am that nigga, I am that nigga
From wayward steps that guide my motion
Provoking my loins to lead the way
Into passionate cries obtained by lies
Overwhelmed by lust that lurks in disguise
Deception is my weapon even against my self
Words spew out detrimental to one's health
In a vacuum of curses, baby mamas and stolen time
Where the concrete witnesses the pain of distrust
Self-esteem is a handicap for my devilish goals
Bent over self-image doggy style to find the hole
From titties to ass to dicks and balls
From circumcised tips to loose vaginal walls
My logic is unclear my lust is relentless
My third eye is clouded can I get a muthafuckin witness
I'm a product of my thinking here is the evidence
Remnants of broken families designed by my deceptive
intelligence
I'm lying to myself so you don't stand a chance
Because my movements are dictated by what's in my pants
My appetite is tenacious spreading legs to provide
That sexual release that my ego justified
Well everybody does it and it feels so good
While fatherless children lurk our neighborhoods
Wanting pleasure without pain oral without obligation
Decimating the future with my dick generation after generation
I am that nigga!!!

1
THE FIRST TIME

The moment had come. Julani for the first time was about to experience something that had alluded him for all these years. Her body was so sexy he anxiously gasped for breath. Her skin was a dark caramel complexion that glowed and accentuated her smooth frame. Her small waist complimented her round beautiful bottom. Her perky breast poked out of her half shirt forming around her nipples. Her big juicy lips were thick and luscious and inviting, as though they wanted to kiss every part of his body. He was nervous trying to maintain an air of arrogance. How dare he let this woman know how much he was excited? He couldn't give her the satisfaction. But since the eyes are the windows to the soul she could tell how bad he wanted her. She seductively curled her index finger for him to follow her to the back bedroom. He followed behind her in a trance being lustfully led by his lower desires. She wore sweat pants but her apple protruded through the loosely fitted sweats. They looked as though two puppy dogs were fighting in her pants as she walked.

It was pure luck how they would eventually meet. He and his buddy Jeff were walking home from their High School Sophomore basketball game. Jeffrey was about five foot eight inches tall, light complexion with a curly top. He never had a problem pulling girls. In fact, sometimes women came up to talk to him. Julani being five foot nine inches always carried himself as a shy guy. He had a darker complexion and was a handsome young man with dimples when he smiled. He would frequently get compliments from women on his pretty smile. But Julani suffered from self-esteem issues. He always assumed that girls didn't really like him. He would show disdain for that which he thought he couldn't have. But at sixteen years of age his hormones were running rampant.

It began with two girls driving into the liquor store parking lot. The girl driving made eye contact with Jeffrey. Without hesitation Jeffrey walked up to the car as if he knew her his entire life. That was always amazing to Julani how Jeffrey could do that so easily. Jeffrey opened up the door for the pretty young woman.

"What is on you ladies' agenda tonight?" Jeffrey began

His aura of confidence emanated all around him. He gave them that golden smile and the driver was hooked.

"We just were picking up a few things from the store. What are ya'll getting into tonight?" The driver replied.

"We were hoping to spend some time to get to know you ladies. What is your name?" Jeffrey continued.

"My name is Sherise and this is my homegirl Terri."

"I'm Jeffrey but you can call me Jeff. This is my homeboy Julani acting all shy and shit." He pointed behind himself with his thumb.

"Well Jeff, we gon' be chilling at the house with my older sister. If you wanna hook up later on we can." Sherise replied.

"Okay, but I need your phone number so that we connect later on. Or we can roll with you now to hang out." Jeff persisted.

"Well that's the thing; if you come you have to bring someone for my older sister. She's going to throw salt in all our game if she doesn't have someone for herself." Sherise explained.

"That's cool, if you slide me the number I'll get another one of my homeboys and we will make this happen in about an hour."

Sherise gave Jeff the number and they went into the liquor store. It was Friday night, which made it perfect to have a good time. It worked out beautifully in Jeff's eyes.

"Look Julani, you gon' fuck with her homegirl and I'll call up Bruce for her older sister."

"Her homegirl was looking good. But Bruce is the same age as us; her sister won't mess with his young ass." Julani sneered.

"How do you know? Quit hating my nigga, let Bruce spit his own game and see how everything goes."

Jeffrey already planned to spend the night at Julani's house. He had a change of clothes already laid out if they got into something. He was kind of glad that the girls said later on. He wanted to shower up and put on his favorite cologne. After all he had been playing basketball for the last two hours. They quickly called Bruce up to see if he was down to roll. Bruce was sixteen but his father had given him this old school mustang that he kept with a fresh paint and polish. Jeff told him about the three girls and he agreed to meet them at Julani's house. It didn't take any time for Bruce to make it to the house. He was there in about ten minutes. Julani had just gotten out the shower when Bruce rung the doorbell.

Jeff got off the phone with the girls when Bruce walked in. Once he wrote down the address he was ready to jump in the shower. After about an hour everyone was dressed and ready to meet up with the girls. They all quickly climbed inside Bruce's Mustang and sped to Sherise's house. Sherise and her sister stayed in a duplex that their parents owned. Their parents stayed in the front house while Sherise and her sister stayed in the back house. It was perfect timing for them to hook up because Sherise's parents had gone out of town.

On the way Bruce had some concerns that he wanted to address up front. Bruce wanted to know how the girls looked.

"The two we saw were fine as hell. But the one I'm messing with was the finest. Her name was Sherise. Lani is probably going to mess with her friend Terri. She looks good too. We are hooking you up with her big sister. I don't know her name." Jeff explained.

"How does she look?" Bruce asked. You could hear skepticism in his tone.

"I don't know because she wasn't with them at the liquor store." Jeff replied.

"Aw hell nah. She could be ugly as hell. I can't take that chance." Bruce gawked.

"What do you mean, you can't take that chance?" Jeff asked.

"Like I said nigga, I can't take that chance. Since you got at Sherise she is yours but Terri is fair game. Matter of fact Julani should fuck with the older sister. The way I see it Julani should take the chance if the girl is to the curb. See you provided the hook up

11

in the first place. So you get first dibs at the girl you wanted to talk to. But I'm providing the vehicle so I should get second dibs."

"Alright I'm cool with that. I'll get at her older sister." Julani replied.

Truthfully Julani didn't think much of the hook up anyway. He had enough confidence to make conversation with the girl but that was about it. Now he figured that he could keep the older sister occupied while Bruce and Raymond got their groove on. Bruce had it in his mind that her being an older woman would make the chances slim for him to really connect. That was his real concern but he didn't relay that to Jeff and Julani.

They made it to Sherise's house about ten minutes after their heated discussion. Sherise opened the door with a smile that warmed Jeff's heart. Terri stood next to her smiling just the same. Jeff introduced Terri to Bruce and there was an instant mutual attraction. They walked through the living room and into the den. The apartment was huge to be a back house duplex. The living room was decorated in royal blue. The matching drapes elegantly blended in with the furniture. The carpet also was royal blue with a silver and blue throw rug lying under the coffee table.

When they made it to the den Sherise's older sister was sitting on the couch watching TV. It became painfully obvious that she and Sherise were sisters because they were both beautiful with very similar features. Since she was sitting down Julani couldn't tell if she had a cute shape or not. He could tell that she had a small waist because she had on a half shirt. She shook his hand as he sat next to her. Everyone else was preoccupied while they made their introduction.

"My name is Julani. But you can call me Lani."

"My name is Shayla but most people just call me Shay."

"So you like watching the Bundys?" He referred to the television program 'Married with Children'.

"Yeah, Al Bundy be having me rolling. I laugh hard off this shit."

"Me too. That is the funniest thing on television."

"You got a pretty ass smile Lani." Shay flirted

"Thank you. You are fine as hell yourself." Julani boldly replied. He felt like he could relax since this beautiful older woman wouldn't have given him the time of day anyway. Let me at least be her friend he thought.

"Thank You. What, you go to my sister's high school?"

"Nah, I stay on the East Side we just saw them at the liquor store. My homeboy Jeff was digging your sister and that is how we hooked up."

"So you're from the other side of town. That is why I have never seen you around here. I would have noticed your chocolate ass. You want something to drink?"

"Yeah, whatever you got."

She got up from the couch and Julani's mouth dropped to the floor. Shay had an backside that would make any man's knees buckle. Julani really needed something to drink because the lust had gotten thick on his tongue. As she walked into the kitchen he briefly went out of his trance. Suddenly he noticed his homeboys looking at Shay's ass. Sherise and Terri had nice shapes but they were nowhere near as voluptuous as Shay. He glanced over at Bruce and he could see the envy in his eyes. Terri was fine but not like Shay. They didn't pay her any attention until she got up from the couch.

She came back to the couch with two glasses of lemonade. She smiled at Julani as she handed him his drink. It smelled like she had put a little bit of gin in his drink.

"You like alcohol?" She rhetorically asked assuming he did.

"Yeah, that's cool!"

"Why don't we go chill in my room and watch TV?"

"O-O-Okay!" Julani stuttered in surprise.

Julani followed Shay into her room giving him an opportunity to take a glance back at Jeff and Bruce. They both were shell shocked to see where she was taking him. Julani glanced back pretending to be sure of himself but secretly he was sweating bullets.

She closed the door behind him. Her room was burgundy and beige. In the middle of the room was a queen-sized bed draped in a burgundy bedspread. They both sat down on her bed and finished their drink. Julani was happy just to be alone in the same room with the sexy twenty-year-old woman. She quickly finished her drink then cut on the television. She lied down on her stomach so that Julani could have a full view her round ass. She was seducing the young man with subtle gestures and movements. He wanted to touch her so bad. But he continued to sip on his gin and juice. Finally he asked her if he could lie down next to her.

"Sure, you can do whatever you want." She smiled.

The tone in her voice had his nature rising to the point where he had to lie on his stomach to hide the bulge coming through his pants. She knew he was having a fit trying to control himself. As he lied down she rolled over to her side so that her ass could gently rub against his leg. Julani found himself face to face with Shay. There was nothing left to do but kiss her.

They began kissing slowly and passionately. Their tongues danced around each other like two Latin lovers engulfed in the Salsa. Julani couldn't believe what was happening to him. She was touching him in all the right places. He felt like he was about to explode. Then suddenly she stopped.

She pushed him off of her then got up from the bed. Yet disappointed Julani still felt a sense of contentment. He never expected to get this far with Shayla. She smiled at him seductively, her eyes glued into his. Slowly she took off her half shirt. Her pretty breasts sat up perky exposing her golden brown nipples. Then she unloosed the knot in her sweats and let them drop to the floor. She stood in front of him with nothing on but a thong. Slowly he stood up admiring her phenomenal figure. His mouth had dropped a long time ago. She was amazing with clothes on. She was astounding without her clothes. As he took off his clothes she took off her last particle of clothing. Julani trembled as the thong hit the floor.

He walked over to her, his dick hard as Chinese arithmetic. Their tongues began to wrestle as their naked bodies touched. She took him by the hand and led him to her queen-sized bed. She lied on her back and quickly spread her legs with her knees propped up.

Julani hesitated for a brief moment then climbed on the bed. His mouth opened again then he gave a low moan when he penetrated. They entangled their bodies together with passion and pain. Julani and Shay embraced one another like two lone souls lost in the moment. Julani was completely overwhelmed in this heavenly pleasure. He felt so good that he began to believe that he was in a dream world. But it was too real to be a dream. Shay on the other hand couldn't believe that a sixteen year old was making her feel so good. He was going so hard and steady that she felt herself cum. After several hard thrusts from Julani she felt the full magnitude of an orgasm.

"Let's do another position!" Shay whispered.

She climbed on the edge of the bed bending over in front of him while he stood up. Her plump round ass bounced hard against his pelvis. The excitement for him was overwhelming. He had broken out in a cold sweat. His body was going through changes that he had never felt before. He couldn't stop pushing inside her harder and harder. What kind of feeling was this that made his entire body tremble? Tears welled up in his eyes. But he wasn't crying in a bad way but a joyous cry unto the Lord. His eyes began to water and finally it came. He started to feel his dick release fluids that it had never released before. Shay must have felt it also because she lied on her stomach. It felt like the entire planet was experiencing a major 10.0 Richter scale earthquake. He had never experienced such a feeling in his entire life. For the first time Julani had experienced an orgasm. Sex felt too good to be real, but it was real.

Julani walked out of the room in a daze. His eyes glazed over everyone in the den with a dense haziness. He was awe-stricken by the moment. Bruce and Jeffrey looked over at him as though he had just won the championship of the world. Julani felt like a man. The pleasure was there but the pain hadn't come yet.

2
CONQUERED

Julani dwelled on that wonderful night with Shay for two weeks. Until he couldn't fight the urge anymore; so he finally built up the nerve to visit her. Not wanting to appear as a stalker he went back and forth about his decision. His desire to see her again overcame his fear of embarrassment. He left basketball practice early that day so that he could ditch Jeff. He made up a story about having to run a few errands for his mother. If he had told Jeff the truth his best friend would have tried to talk him out of it.

He caught two buses to Shay's house not knowing if she was home. He arrived around four in the afternoon. He reluctantly walked to the side of her house and into the back yard. He hesitated for a moment briefly forgetting they didn't have a dog. He walked up to her front door took a deep breath then finally built up the nerve to knock.

"Who is it?" A woman yelled from inside.

He hesitated.

"Who is it, I said?" The voice sounded as if it had drawn closer and more irritated.

"Julani!" he replied.

For a moment the woman behind the door paused and everything was silent. Then she opened the door. Shay answered the door smiling. She had her hair in a ponytail with golden brown highlights. She had on a light blue sweater and a jean mini-skirt. She didn't have any shoes on showing her meticulously pedicure toes. Julani felt the desire for her intensify as she once again captivated him with her beauty.

"Where are you coming from?" She asked while letting him in.

"From my school."

16

"Somebody dropped you off?"

"Nah, I caught a couple of buses."

"But you didn't even know if I was here. You should have called to see if I was home." She sighed.

"You never gave me your phone number."

"Well I will be sure to do that before you leave. Did you forget something is that why you came way over here?"

"Nah, I came to see you."

"You caught two buses just to come see me? That's sweet. Come here so I can give you a kiss." She smiled.

He slowly met her half way until they were face to face. He stared at her pretty face and gently kissed her on the lips.

"Thank you for coming by, sometimes I get a little lonely in this place."

"What about your sister, doesn't she live back here with you?"

"Yeah but she is into her thing and I'm into mine. She has a lot of after school activities. She wants to go to Howard University to be a lawyer. As for me I'm going to school to do hair. When I get out of school I come home. You want something to drink?" Julani eyed her walking into the kitchen.

"Yeah sure, thank you."

"Anyway, sometimes I get bored with my routine. I don't go out that much so I appreciate company."

"I'll come by as much as you would like me to." Julani eagerly replied.

"You are so sweet! I wish more guys were like you." She smiled while handing him lemonade.

"You didn't put any alcohol in it this time." Julani said.

"Yeah, that was for us to mellow out that night. Now that we are just kicking it and we know each other I don't have to get you drunk." She chuckled.

She sat right next to him on the couch. Her perfume was intoxicating. He felt like taking her in his arms that very moment. His fear of rejection held back his urge.

"So you want to be my new friend?" She asked.

17

"Yeah, I want to be your friend."

She leaned in with her eyes closed connecting her lips to his. They began wrestling around on the couch exchanging passionate kisses. Her slow moans aroused Julani. Once again she lifted him up so that she could lead him to her bedroom. Julani loved how she took control.

In a matter of seconds they were totally naked. She started to gently massage and pull on his manhood with slow deliberate strokes. She began kissing on his neck all the way down his torso. Her thick lips wrapped around his penis. He moaned. He felt the blood rush through his loins. She must have felt it too because she stopped.

"Nah, baby it ain't time for you to cum yet." She whispered.

She lied on her back while still holding on to him. Shayla epitomized sexuality. She made every bone in his body ache for her touch. He had never felt like this before. He felt heaven all over again. Instead of fast and hard she had him moving nice and slow. It was a change for Julani but felt just as good. She touched him on every part of his body with her soft manicured hands. He grabbed her ass with both hands while she continued to caress him. His head was face down in the pillow still stroking at a slow pace. This was the woman of his dreams he imagined. She made sure that he felt her in every inch of his body. Then that feeling came again. The one that he had the last time he was with Shay. His entire body soaked from sweat. Feeling him about to cum she whispered into his ear.

"Let it go baby, let it go."

At this point Julani's mouth was wide open. He was sweating so hard that it was dripping on Shay's breasts and face. She continues to grab his ass as if the sweat was making her hornier. Without any more strength he exploded inside of her. With several final thrusts he finally collapsed.

Shay got up from the bed and grabbed washcloths for the both of them. As she wet both washcloths she yelled into the room for Julani.

"Come wash up Lani"

They stood in the bathroom together helping one another wash up. Once Shay was done with herself she began washing Julani as though he was her child. But she made him feel like a man.

"Next time we do something I want to teach you something, okay?" She said.

"What's that?"

"I want you to learn how to lick a woman's vagina. Have you ever done that before?"

"No, I have never done that before. But I will try it if you want me to." He eagerly replied.

"Well we will try it next time but not this time. I just want to sit and watch TV with you for now. Hopefully you will be back over to see me soon." She gently touched his face.

"I can come over tomorrow if you like."

"Nah, I got something to do. But you can come over Thursday about the same time."

They both sat and watched television until Shay's sister Sherise got home. Shay lied across the couch with her head on his lap. They were bonding in their own sensual way.

"How have you been doing Julani? I was just about to call Jeff when I got in. What are you doing way on this part of town?"

"Oh he forgot something? I'm about to give him a ride home in a little bit." Shay interjected before Julani could respond.

Shay quickly got up from the couch and grabbed her car keys. Julani followed her out to the Volkswagen parked on the street.

"So we are rolling in your sisters' car?"

"Nigga please, this is my car. I let her borrow it to go to the store that day ya'll met her."

"Oh!"

They jumped into Shay's Volkswagen and sped off. They didn't have much conversation because Shay had the music up loud. All she wanted was directions to get to his house. When she pulled up she finally turned the music down.

"Baby, I will be glad to see you on Thursday, okay?" She leaned over to kiss him.

"Yeah, I will see you Thursday." He replied.

He wanted to talk but she gave him the impression that she was ready to leave. Without giving it a second thought he hopped out of the car. He walked around to the driver's side to give her a final kiss. Julani stood in the middle of the street while she drove off watching her turn the corner. He had found the woman of his dreams. He walked into his house and went straight to his room. All he could think about was his new girlfriend Shay. For the first time Julani thought he was in love.

Weeks would go by and they would continue their sex dates. He would catch two buses to see her as usual. She always treated him like a king whenever he went to her house. She would sometimes cook for him when it got too late. She would show him different sexual positions and experiments. She showed him how to go down on a woman. She even told him how it should smell. In his wildest dreams would he have thought that his girlfriend would be a twenty-year-old bombshell? It was nothing Shay could tell him to do that he wouldn't do. His passion for her was dictated by every action he made. He would bring her flowers. He even saved up his money so that he could buy her a charm. This was the happiest he had ever been in his entire life. He even played basketball better than he did before.

One day Julani was able to leave to go to her house earlier than usual. His coach had cancelled basketball practice for the day. Since he didn't get to see her the day before he decided on that day to go to the mall. He had seen some shoes that he thought would look really pretty on her. He inadvertently asked for her shoe size. Making it appear as mere curiosity she answered him. He went to the mall bought the shoes then had them gift-wrapped.

When he made it to her house he knocked on the door but got no response. He knocked on the door again but this time he heard Shay yelling 'just a minute'. He grew exceedingly eager now that his baby was coming to the door. Just to see her made him feel good inside. She cracked the door open without allowing him to see inside. She didn't invite him when she poked her head out the door. Instead she walked outside and closed the door behind her.

"I thought we said you would call before you came by, Julani. I wasn't expecting you so early."

"I know, I just wanted to surprise you with this present I bought you." He smiled.

"Oh baby let me see."

He handed her the bag with the box of shoes inside. When she opened the box she saw the prettiest shoes that she could lay her eyes on.

"Oh Julani, these are so pretty. I got an outfit that will go just right with these. You must have been saving up for some time to get these." She smiled.

"I did a few hustles around the neighborhood to get the money together. Nothing illegal of course but I'm glad you like them."

"I love them!" She said while kissing him on the cheek. She usually kissed him on the lips.

He thought it was odd but he ignored his feelings. She then grabbed his arm and started walking him out the backyard and into the street.

"Look baby, we need to talk." She said.

"About what?"

"About you coming over here. We are going to have to put a stop to this."

"Why, I only came over without calling because of the surprise. I won't come over again without calling." Julani blurted out.

"No baby it's not that. See Julani, I'm twenty years old. You are only sixteen years old and eventually that will become a problem. I am going to start wanting to date men that can do things for me. Someone that I can settle down with and have a family. As for you, you have plenty of time to meet a nice young girl and have a long-term relationship. I want to start dating men that can do things that men do. You are still a minor and to tell the truth I can get charged with statutory rape for having sex with you. Besides, as cute as you are, you will have no problem finding a girlfriend after me."

21

"But you are the only girlfriend I have ever wanted or will ever want." Julani pleaded.

"You are saying that now but you haven't even become a man yet. You probably don't know what you want right now." She softly replied, sensing his hurt feelings.

"I know that I want you."

"I feel kind of bad Julani so don't make me feel worse. See you got introduced to sex before you were introduced to love. And that is clouding your judgment because you are infatuated with our sex together. We had good sex together. But we are not in love with each other because we don't really know each other outside of sex."

"This is fucked up Shay. You are breaking my heart. I know how I feel about you sixteen years old or not. I want to be with you and only you."

"We had sex together, baby, that's it; Nothing more nothing less. One of these days you will forget about what we had and move on to truly love another girl. And she will be real lucky to have you. I know I am sure lucky to have you for the time that I did. But Julani it is time for us to both move on." She spoke in a tone of sympathy.

Julani dropped his head because his eyes were filled with water. He never wanted a woman to see him cry. But this was Shay, the woman that taught him how to make love. She taught him how to be confident about his sexuality. Now it was over. Paradise had come to an end. The one woman that had him conquered broke his heart. He couldn't ever let this happen again.

3
BITCHES AIN'T SHIT

There were lingering effects to the heartbreak that Shay gave to Julani. He had to face his fears and deal with his life. If something doesn't kill you it only makes you stronger he was told. He felt that it was time for him to get stronger. He stopped asking Jeff about Shay. Jeff and Sherise were still talking off and on. Jeff wasn't too serious about it because he knew that Sherise was going off to college. So he always had his females on the side. Sherise was fine enough in his opinion to make her his main girl though.

Now that Julani was over Shay, Jeff could take him out to meet new girls. He had tried it once before to help him get over it. But that didn't work. When they met up with the girls Julani only talked about Shay, which spoiled it for Jeff. Because the other girl wasn't with hanging out if her friend wasn't going to be with anyone. And Julani was too depressed to be with anyone. Now that that was over it was time for Julani to turn over a new leaf. Julani had saved up his money and was able to buy a cheap car for six hundred dollars. He picked up Jeff one Saturday afternoon about a week after he bought the car.

"Damn nigga, I'm sure glad that you have gotten over Shay. It's all kinds of bitches you could be hollering at. You stuck on that broad. She is fine then a muthafucka but I ain't getting sprung over any female. It's too many out here to be worried about one." Jeff arrogantly replied.

"There you go on that pimp shit!" Julani retorted.

"Nah nigga, I'm a player not a pimp. I don't share women but they all got to share me. But then again, I do get money from some of them." Jeff chuckled.

"You crazy! Now where are we going?"

"These girls stay in Paramount. Just stay down Orange until you get to Alondra then make a right."

"Where you meet them at?"

"At Magic Mountain when I went with Sherise and her family."

"Nigga you was getting at females when you was with Sherise?" Julani was surprised from audacity.

"Nah, that's the crazy part. They got at me! They told me that they had seen me with my girlfriend but still wanted to hook up. They were waiting for my ass right outside the restroom."

"Where was Sherise when all this was taking place?"

"Her and her cousin went to get on the Goliath. I didn't feel like waiting in the line with them so I told them I would hang back." Jeff laughed.

"Wasn't you with Bruce and Terri?"

"Yeah, but that fat ass nigga Bruce think he's in love. Him and Terri went off somewhere. I was all by myself." Jeff slyly replied.

"All of ya'll was able to fit in Bruce's mustang?"

"Hell nah, Shay let Sherise use her Volkswagen bug. I think she had some nigga coming over or something." Jeff accidentally blurted out.

"Yeah, probably the same nigga that was over there when I came by with those new shoes." Julani sneered.

"Probably so! But don't even trip because the girl I hooked you up with got a big ole ass." Jeff replied.

"For real? How does she look in the face?"

"She's cute, but you gon' probably think she is the bomb. She told me that she likes dark niggas. I even had one for Bruce's fat ass but that nigga so sprung over Terri he ain't thinking about another girl. She got that nigga on a leash." Jeff teased.

"Real talk?" Julani agreed.

"Yeah, he walks her through the mall, carrying bags and shit. I seen the nigga do it. Don't get me wrong I like Sherise a whole lot but she won't be dictating my every movement. That nigga's whole life is scheduled around Terri."

24

"I thought he said that he was Mister Mack Daddy?" Julani replied.

"Well now that nigga is a Simp. Turn at this light."

They turned on this quiet neighborhood block in the suburbs. It looked peaceful and serene. They pulled up in front of a beige house with brown trimming. They made sure they had their breath mints and everything looked in place. They walked up to the door side by side like they were Siamese twins. It took Jeff ringing the doorbell twice before someone answered.

Finally a pretty caramel complexioned girl comes to the door. She was about five foot four inches tall. She had pretty dimples when she smiled. Her hair was almost shoulder length in a conservative hairstyle. Her tightly fitted jeans showed that she was an athletic girl. Just the way Jeff liked.

"Good to see you made it Jeffrey. Come on in! This must be your friend. Ooh Deidre is going to like him a lot." Marsha said.

Julani smiled when she said that.

"And he got dimples too." She added.

"Damn, Marsha you act like you want him and done forgot about me." Jeff feigned jealousy.

"I could never forget your cute self. But I know what Deidre likes and she is going to like him. What is your name?" Marsha pinched Jeff's cheek.

"Julani but most people call me Lani for short." Julani confidently replied.

"Girl come out here, he's cute!" Marsha yelled in the room for Deidre.

Deidre came walking out of the bedroom smiling. She was a pretty light skinned girl with skinny legs and a round backside. Her waist was small with small perky breast. Her tight jeans hugged her butt as if they were painted on. She even walked like she was slightly pigeon toed. Her hair was slicked back in a ponytail that was neatly cropped. She walked up to Julani and shook his hand.

"Damn girl, you ain't lying he is cute." Deidre confirmed.

"You are fine as hell yourself." Julani replied.

That was how they met. So from that day forward Julani and Deidre became a couple. He was really digging his new girlfriend. There was only one problem. He didn't trust her. He never was really an extremely jealous guy but it was there. He was one of those types of men that didn't show that he was jealous. But everywhere Julani and Deidre went he would catch stares. Men would even make loud comments like.

"Damn, she got a big ole ass!"

"I'll fuck the shit out of her!"

"That nigga ain't hitting that right!"

Deidre would try to reassure Julani that she was with him but he still was bothered by people's remarks. She would always tell him to ignore the comments because Julani would be ready to fight. She had developed feelings for Julani fast. Being totally satisfied by the man she was with she didn't pay other guys any attention. Nevertheless Julani thought that in the long run she might break his heart. Deidre was haunted by the damage that Shay had caused.

One day their relationship had to jump a real hurdle. It started with Deidre going out with her friends one night. She, Marsha and two other girlfriends decided to go to the movies, dinner and the arcade. They made arrangements this particular weekend because Julani and Jeff had two tickets to the Lakers game. Deidre wasn't trying to catch but whenever she went outside she looked fabulous. Bruce just so happened to be out with Terri when he seen her with her friends. They all met on a double date before. Deidre wasn't doing anything wrong but guys were all over her. Everywhere she went guys were trying to talk to her. One guy was so persistent that he tried to slide his number in Deidre's mini-skirt pocket.

"What are you doing nigga; I told you I got a man?" She snapped.

"Why ain't that nigga with you now, if you were my woman I wouldn't never let yo fine ass get away." He flirted.

"That's why you ain't my man." Deidre fired back.

Bruce and Terri were witnessing this take place from afar. The arcade was too loud for anyone to hear what he or she was saying. All Bruce knew was that the guy was getting too close. Too close Bruce believed for her to be his homeboy's lady. He decided to walk over there. But Terri stopped him and told him to mind his business. She quickly pulled him from out of the arcade.

The next day Bruce called up Julani to tell him the bad news. It was typical for Bruce to put extras on any situation. As fragile as Julani was emotionally it didn't help his relationship with Deidre.

"Yeah man, I saw your lady at the arcade with her homegirls the other night. Some nigga was all up on her grabbing her ass and everything dog."

"Nigga you're bullshitting?" Julani snarled.

"Real talk, my nigga. I don't know if she was throwing him play or not but he was too close not to be getting play. I felt I had to tell you dog or that would be fucked up. I was about to go over there and check that nigga but Terri wouldn't let me go."

"Aw nigga you gon' let your girl stop you from checking a nigga that is trying to holler at my girl?" Julani flared up at Bruce.

"You are the nigga that should be checking his girl. She's wearing tight ass mini-skirts and having niggas grab her ass. I got everything under control with Terri but Deidre is the one in question homie." Bruce taunted.

"What are you trying to say fool?" Julani replied.

"Don't get mad at me Lani get mad at your girl or the game, my nigga." Bruce remarked.

Julani hung up the phone in his face. Bruce chuckled to himself after he heard the dial tone. Julani was angry but he knew his misdirected anger should be towards Deidre. If he was going to get mad at anyone it should be her. He called her house but the phone kept ringing. He decided against leaving a message on her parent's home phone. So he decided to call up Marsha's house to see if she was over there.

"Hello!"

"Hello, can I speak to Marsha?"

"This is Marsha, who is this?"

"This is Julani. Marsha is Deidre over there?"

"No, but she should be walking up in about ten or fifteen minutes, why what's up."

"Just tell her that I am on my way over your house to talk to her."

"Okay, but is everything alright?"

"Yeah, I just need to talk to her."

Julani drove over to Marsha's house rehearsing how he was going to put Deidre in check. He was going to break down to her how his lady shouldn't be close to any nigga. But he knew that he couldn't get too upset until he heard her side of the story. Besides Bruce's fat ass could have been exaggerating he considered. He pulled up in front of Marsha's house and saw Deidre waiting on the porch for him. She had a perplexed look on her face. Deidre had it already in her mind what Julani was rushing over there for. She knew Bruce seen her the other night at the arcade. It was no telling what Bruce told Julani. She slowly walked down the walkway to greet him at the car.

"How are you doing baby, Marsha said that you had to speak to me?" She half-heartedly smiled.

"Yeah, Bruce told me he saw you the other night. Some nigga was grabbing your ass and all up on you." Julani retorted.

"It was a nigga all up on me but he didn't grab my ass. That's a lie!" Deidre fired back.

"Why are you letting some nigga be all up on you Deidre? That's fucked up." Julani asked. Deidre could hear the hurt in his tone.

"I didn't let him be all up on me. He wouldn't leave me alone. I told his punk ass I had a man but he wouldn't stop. He kept on me so much that I told my friends that we needed to go." She explained.

"What the hell were you wearing to make a nigga be on you like that?"

"I had on that jean mini-skirt that looks like it's cut at the bottom. With my beige halter top and some sandals, why?"

"That tight ass mini-skirt you wore to the picnic?"

"Yeah, why?"

"You going out with a bunch of your homegirls and you got on a tight ass mini-skirt and you don't think niggas won't harass you? Come on now you know better than that. You were trying to get niggas to jock you." Julani insisted.

"Not to sound conceited Lani baby, but niggas jock me all the time. Whatever I wear I still have guys trying to holler but I tell them I am with you." She replied calmly.

"But you ain't got to advertise sex all the time. You were embarrassing me in front of my homies."

"Bruce ain't your friend, that nigga is a snake. You can't trust him anyway." She fired back.

"But I should totally trust you, huh?" Julani sarcastically replied.

"Do what you feel in your heart." Deidre replied. She turned her back on him trying to hide her pain. She was hurt and insulted by his sarcasm.

"That's why niggas say bitches ain't shit." Julani mumbled under his breath.

"What, now you calling me a bitch? No nigga I'm your lady and I've been true to that. The bitch was that girl Shay that dogged you out not me. All I ever did was love yo insecure ass. You know what…"

Deidre stopped in mid sentence and walked away. She was trying to hold back her tears. She really loved him but he just was too crazy to see. He seen her walk away and he wanted to call her back. At that moment he realized that he loved her.

"Deidre, Deidre, I'm sorry, come back so we can talk about it." He pleaded

"That's going to have to be on another day Julani because I ain't in a good mood to talk to you right now. Maybe Tomorrow."

Julani saw her walk inside Marsha's house and all he could do was put his head down. His words hurt her as well as they hurt him.

4
TRIFLING

It took about four or five days before Deidre even spoke to Julani. He would call but she would ignore his phone calls. Finally on the fourth day late at night she accepted his call.

"Hello?"

"Hello, Julani it's me!"

"How are you doing baby?"

"I'm doing fine, how are you?"

"Baby I fucked up real bad, let me make it up to you. I know I should trust you and I'm sorry about everything I said."

"I believe you, and I have been missing you."

"I missed you too."

They talked on the phone until the wee hours of the night. She really missed him and felt that he had suffered long enough. They agreed to meet after school so that they could spend time together. Julani left his high school early so that he could pick her up from hers. He was already outside when she came out of the school gate. She couldn't help but smile from ear to ear seeing her man waiting for her. She climbed inside the car looking at him as though she was in a daze. They intimately embraced one another and began passionately kissing. They acted as if they hadn't seen each other in years. After endless moments of intimacy they slowly started to loosen their embrace of one another. As they were letting each other go someone inadvertently yelled.

"That's a lucky ass nigga!"

But Julani didn't care what anyone said because his girl was with him. His mother had gone to Las Vegas for the week so they had the place to themselves. They quickly jumped in the shower once they made it to his house. They stayed in the shower for a while playing with the soap and water. They laughed and joked about friends and family. She would look into his eyes with her hands on his chest. He would wrap his arms around her waist with his fingers on her butt. Their bond had become solidified as they stood in the shower making love to one another.

Julani got out the shower and helped Deidre get out as well. Then he slowly dried her off with his towel. He then went into his mother's room to get some of his mother's Neutrogena Body Oil. He poured a little on his hand and began caressing the center of her hand. He then slowly started caressing her arms and shoulders. With each stroke he was slow and deliberate. He went on to rubbing oil on her breast while he licked her belly button. The passion began to intensify. Julani started rubbing the Body Oil up and down her legs and thighs. Then he started massaging her feet as he slid his finger through her soft pretty pedicure toes. As he rubbed the palm of her feet she began to purr. She was feeling hot all over. His erotic strokes began to touch pressure points that made her surrender to his every suggestion.

He then put his mouth on her clitoris. He used his tongue with smooth strokes as his lips continued to suck on her pearl. She gave him a moan that assured him that she was enjoying his mouth. As his tongue stroked her vagina she went into a trance. She was feeling the passion of his mouth and she couldn't control herself. She began to slowly squirm on his bed as her legs went in many different directions. She felt the perspiration all over her body. His hot tongue passionately stroked her vagina, as she exploded with ecstasy. He didn't stop.

She slowly pulled him up to her face so that she could look into his eyes. He took his penis and gently rubbed it against her clitoris. Her body squirmed. Then he penetrated with one hard thrust. She shrieked indicating the joy she felt from the pleasure pain. His strokes were slow and deep as they both developed a compatible rhythm. Both tried to touch every part of one another's body. She had her hands on his buttocks as his arm extended up her back and onto her shoulder. She could not believe that she was being made to feel so good. It was literally paradise for this young inexperienced woman. She moaned at every stroke as Julani picked up his intensity.

Was this love that made her feel so good? It must be love that made her feel like paradise had touched every inch of her body. Deidre was feeling her entire body sweat in this pool of ecstasy. She began to cry and as tears fell from her face she realized a joy she has never experienced before. Her body trembled in explosive ecstasy. As she trembled she began to understand what she was experiencing. This was truly breathtaking. Julani began to moan loudly as well. One loud moan indicated that he also reached a wonderful climax.

Julani rolled over to lie next to her on the bed. They both were still looking at one another eye to eye. He slowly caressed her pretty face with his finger. Another tear fell from her eye.

"Julani, I have never felt that way in my life. Baby you made me feel so good. I love you so much." Deidre admitted.

"Baby I love you too, I want to share my life with you Deidre."

They continued to hold each other in bed without saying a word. They both lied totally naked in a full embrace of one another. After an hour they got up from the bed so that Julani could cook something to eat. He cooked a full meal as they sat on the couch and watched television. They both felt that life would be heaven if every day were like this. Julani then broke out the Connect Four game so that they could play for a little while. Back and forth they would win games against one another until they both agreed that it was getting late. In truth, neither of them wanted the night to end.

"Why don't you spend the night Friday? My mother doesn't get back from Las Vegas until Sunday. I know your friend Marsha can cover for you." Julani asked.

"Okay, but you're going to have to pick me up from school. Which means you will have to leave school early like you did today?" Deidre suggested.

"Okay, I'm a junior so I can miss classes a little more nowadays."

Reluctantly it was time for Julani to take his lady home. They drove to her house and sat in the car and talked for a while. They kissed each other goodbye as Julani watched his woman walk into her house. He made it home in twenty minutes flat. Being on cloud nine he watched television until he heard the phone ring. He jumped up assuming it was Deidre. He looked on the caller ID.

"What's up Jeff Dog, how you living my nigga?"

"Damn nigga, you sound happy as hell. Deidre must have forgiven yo ass."

"Real talk! I'm glad too because I just took her home and we had a good time together."

"Did you hit?"

"Man, I ain't about to get into that shit nigga that's my lady. Not a broad off the street." Julani chuckled.

"You must've hit as happy as you sound." Jeff pried.

"So what's up, what are you into?" Julani changed the subject. He didn't want to demean Deidre in that way.

"I'm chilling; I wanted to know what you were into?"

"Man I'm relaxing at the house watching TV. You wanted to shoot through and hang out for awhile?"

"I'll do you one better. I got this female that stays on the West Side that's fine as hell. She wants to hook up tonight but I haven't got a place to bring her. And since yo mom is out of town…?"

"Yeah, that's cool but don't fuck up my mom's sheets. In fact, nigga use a sheet to put over my moms' bed."

"That's cool, but nigga she was telling me she got her cousin that's coming with her."

"I got a girl." Julani replied.

"Nigga I know, Mr. Faithful. All I'm asking is that you run a little interference. Keep her cousin company while I'm in the room with her."

"Alright that's cool, when you coming through?"

"In about thirty to forty-five minutes. That will give you time to clean up and wash up if you know what I mean."

"Whatever man, I'll see you in a little bit."

Julani got off the phone with Jeff and started cleaning up. He had to wash dishes and straighten up the living room. Since it was only Deidre and his dishes he took about ten minutes to straighten up. He burned some incense that his mother hated. She only allowed him to burn them in his room. But since he had the entire house to himself he burned it everywhere. He did a quick vacuum and jumped in the shower. He was afraid that he smelled like sex and perfume. Even though he had a lady he wasn't going to make a bad impression on the girl coming over. He threw on one of his sweat suits and watched television. He almost dozed off when he heard the doorbell ring. He slowly got up from his slumber and walked over to the door.

"Who is it?"

"Who do you think it is nigga, open up?" Jeff clowned.

He opened the door to see Jeff eagerly barging through the door. Following behind him was a beautiful chocolate woman that made Julani say to himself.

"Damn!"

Seeing that she was athletic he knew that she was for Jeff. Then the other girl walked in looking like Gabrielle Union when she played in 'Deliver Us from Eva'. As she walked into the house he realized that her ass was still coming around the corner. She had the biggest butt that he had ever seen. Her backside was so big that it appeared as though a comic book artist had drawn her it. Julani was simply devastated by the weight that she carried behind her. It was bigger than both Shay and Deidre's Asses. She wore a long dress to try and down play her booty but she couldn't help it. To add insult to injury she had a small waist that appeared as though Julani could put his hands together around her waist. For an instance the air got thinner. Jeff knew that Julani was into big asses so this was a set up. At least Julani felt that way.

He greeted everyone and led everyone into the living room where the television was already on. He asked everyone did they want anything to eat or drink. The girls were thirsty so he went into the kitchen and he indicated that Jeff followed. Once they made it inside the kitchen Julani began to whisper.

"Why would you set me up with a girl with an ass like that? Nigga you trying to get me in trouble." Julani snapped at Jeff.

"Nah, man I never seen her until tonight. Actually that's her cousin who stays in San Pedro. I met this girl at the Lakewood mall." Jeff admitted.

"She wasn't with her when you got at her?" Julani asked.

"Nah, she was with her mom but her mom was in another store. She slid me the number and we hooked up for the first time tonight. I have been talking to her over the phone for about a week. She likes talking that sex shit real tough over the phone so I wanted to find out if she is true to her word. I didn't know that she would have a cousin built like that."

"I'm gon' try to be cool but damn, that's a big ole ass." Julani admitted.

"I know, I know."

They walked back in with everyone's drink in their hand.

"I'm being rude I forgot to introduce everybody. This is my homeboy Julani. This nigga is my best friend and my road dog. This pretty young lady's name is Lanette, and I don't remember your name."

"My name is Lisa!" She replied.

Julani sat next to her while Jeff sat next to Lanette. They began to laugh and talk in a real good vibe. The atmosphere was relaxed and jovial. About twenty minutes in Jeff and Lanette went into the other room. Now it got a little uncomfortable for Julani who was sitting next to this big booty bombshell.

"Just you and yo mama live here?" Lisa asked. She wanted to make small talk because she thought he was cute.

"Yeah, but my mother went to Las Vegas for the whole week."

"That's what Jeff was telling us on the way over here. That's cool that ya'll grew up together and still hang with each other."

"Yeah, that's my boy; we go way back like fat crayons."

"Where is your bathroom?" She stood up.

"Down the hallway, it's the first door on your right."

35

She got up from the couch and stretched. She made sure that she arched her ass out so that Julani could get a look at how big it was. He stared at her ass out the corner of his eye. She also looked out the corner of her eye to see if he was looking. His dick had already gotten hard just from her standing up. She slowly walked into the hallway switching her hips so that her ass could bounce through the dress. Once she disappeared from sight Julani did a fake faint from admiring her booty. She stayed in the bathroom for about thirty seconds then walked out with her face wet.

"It's hot up in here you got an air conditioner?"

"Nah, but you can get as comfortable as you like." Julani replied

"I can take off anything I like?"

"Yeah, anything you like."

"This dress is getting kind of hot; I wanted to take that off if that is okay? I only got a thong on under this dress." She teased.

"Yeah." Julani said as if he meant to say 'hell yeah'.

"You want to help me take it off?"

When she said that Julani knew that she wanted to give him some ass. He moved over closer to her on the couch. While still sitting he unzipped the dress slowly. He helped her pull the dress down from over hips and ass. As the dress was coming off and he seen it up close and bare, he truly seen how big her ass really was. He couldn't help but touch it. It was big, jiggely yet firm. He never seen an ass that big, especially naked. He had to touch it again. This time he rubbed on her ass nice and smooth. He then uses his hand to lift her booty cheeks up. She didn't move or resist. In fact she pushed her ass closer to his face.

He turned her around and kissed her belly button. He stood up and they started kissing. He grabbed her ass the entire time they were kissing. Finally he slipped off her thong. Now she stood butt naked with a blouse on. He lifted the blouse from over her head. He doesn't even bother with the bra. He then moves her back to his room. He kept her back to the wall so that he could smoothly knock the picture of Deidre off his dresser. He laid Lisa on the bed and pulled a condom from out of his drawer. At that point he was no longer sensual but lustful; so once the condom was on he slid right inside of her. She moaned as he pushed inside of her time and time again. He was trying to beat it up so bad; she'll be sore for two weeks he pondered. He had her feet almost touching her head. He was plunging hard inside of her like he was auditioning for a porno. But he had to make sure he done something before he busted a nut.

"Let's do it doggy style." Julani blurted out.

Julani quickly turned her over and started pounding from the back. She was bent over on the edge of the bed with her legs on the ground and her hands on the bed. Julani stood behind her with all five fingers dug deep into the meat of her ass. That's when she began to make loud noises. She was feeling him go inside her relentlessly. She was making her ass bounce while he continued to aggressively penetrate. Then she decided to lie on her stomach. Her big booty was poking out and Julani went wild. He lost all control of himself and started going faster and harder. Faster and harder he went. Faster and harder he went. Finally he felt that feeling in his entire body, he was about to cum. He was ready to release and with one final stroke he exploded. He began to tremble like he was going into a seizure and it became obvious to Lisa that he was about to cum. Julani gave a moan and collapsed on top of her.

As he lied next to her it dawned on him that she wasn't Deidre. He had just cheated on Deidre. Now that all the lust was gone and his head was clear he realized his crime. He lied up next to Lisa feeling like he really was pathetic. How could he do Deidre like this? How could he cheat on his lady? As much as he loved Deidre he realized that he was trifling. He had just become a low down dirty dog like his father. At least that is what his mama told him about his daddy. Now he was hurting the woman he loved because he couldn't control his dick. Trifling just trifling.

5
DRAMA

Julani tried to conceal the guilt as much as he could. He felt bad but he would be damned if he admitted his crime to Deidre. In fact, he would try to get away with it as long as possible. He and Lisa exchanged numbers that night. He had to hit the skins a few more times. He couldn't go back on the crime now that he committed it. At least that was how he figured it. He still did everything with Deidre. She was his main girl who he loved and would do anything for; except stay faithful. She couldn't understand how big Lisa's booty was. He just couldn't give up that bomb sex.

Friday came along and Deidre spent the night like she promised. They went to the movies that night and later on went back to Julani's house. She had her cute little leopard skin bag that she carried her clothes in. When he picked her up from school she was wearing brown jeans and a leopard shirt. She had on matching heals that also had leopard skin. She made her ensemble look good and Julani felt proud. But he wasn't proud of himself. Deidre was his first mutual 'first love' and he had already betrayed her. He felt bad and it showed.

"What's wrong with you? You act as if you ain't glad to see me." Deidre said playfully.

"I'm always glad to see you; I just got something on my mind."

"What's on your mind, maybe I can help you with it?" Deidre jovially replied.

"It's nothing, how was your day?" Julani replied.

"It was pretty good I must say. I got an A on my math test, which puts me on the honor roll. I got a bunch of compliments from

38

women about my outfit today. And that shit doesn't happen. I very seldom get compliments from women unless it's Marsha or something. Bitches hate on each other."

"Yeah that's true most women don't get along with each other. My mama is beefing with her sisters all the time. I'll be like, Mama, Aunt Sheryl called and she will say she's not talking to Aunt Sheryl. What's up with that?"

"Shit, I don't know! I try not to do it but girls do it to me all the time." Deidre complained.

"They just are jealous of my Boo, with yo fine ass."

Deidre blushed then playfully hit Julani.

They made it to the movies around eight in the evening. They made it back to Julani's house around ten-thirty. Julani went into his bedroom and took off all his clothes except his boxers. Deidre followed his lead and took off everything but her panties and bra. They sat back, watched television and ate. They watched sitcom after sitcom until Julani started picking at Deidre.

"Quit pushing me punk!" Deidre playfully cried.

"What you gon' do about it?" He teased.

"I'll show you what I'm gon' do about it."

Deidre dived on top of Julani. They began wrestling on the floor. They rolled over on top of each other until they started kissing. The more they kissed the hotter they both became. Julani was already stiff as a rock. Deidre's soft body rubbing against him was even more seductive. He took off her bra and starts sucking her breast. He then slid off her panties. She pulled down his boxers and starts grabbing his penis. She stroked his manhood until he penetrated. They rolled around on the floor making love to one another. The emotions ran high as their sincere love for one another intensified with each moment.

"Turn over so I can do it from the back." Julani asked.

"You gon' stick it in my butt?" Deidre asked. She had a perplexed facial expression.

"Nah baby, it still goes into your vagina just from the backside." Julani smirked.

"Oh okay!"

She turned over so that Julani could do it from the back. He started digging into her real hard while grabbing her ass. She wanted to please him but it began to hurt.

"Baby, don't go so deep, that hurts too much." She whispered.

"Okay!" Julani said.

When he slowed down he realized that he was about to cum. He tried to catch it but he couldn't. He had his orgasm without allowing Deidre to get hers. His guilt was beginning to compound.

"Sorry, baby you didn't get to cum." Julani apologized.

"I had a small one when we were doing it doggy style. But not as big as the first one." She admitted.

"My fault!"

"You weren't acting like you were making love to me Julani. You were going wild like we were in an X-rated movie or something."

"Nah baby I was just trying something new. That's all!" Julani dismissed her observation.

"You watch those pornos, huh, that's why you wanted to try something new? What kind of movies you got." Deidre asked.

"I don't have any dirty movies but I have seen one or two hanging out with Jeff." Julani lied.

In truth he had some under his bed that he had borrowed from Bruce. But he couldn't tell her that because Deidre was his little angel. He didn't want her to think that he was a pervert. He held her tight and closed his eyes as if he was going to sleep. Before they knew it they had both dozed off.

Of course he was more used to the environment so it was easier for him sleep. But Deidre woke up early so that she could call Marsha. She wanted to make sure that her mother didn't call Marsha's house. Once she found out that her mother hadn't called she let Marsha go back to sleep. But when she clicked the phone to hang up she heard someone say Hello.

"Hello, hi is this Julani's mother, my name is Lisa?"

"No, this is Julani's girlfriend, who are you?" Deidre asked.

40

"I said Lisa, and if he was your man we wouldn't have been fucking Wednesday night." Lisa sneered.

"Bitch you lying, because he was with me Wednesday." Deidre fired back.

"He wasn't with you around ten 'o'clock that night because I was over his house. Me, my cousin Lanette and his homeboy Jeff." Lisa fired right back.

Deidre thought about it when she said Jeff. She knew Jeff was a player because he had a girlfriend when he started messing with Marsha. But she didn't want to believe anything some strange bitch had to say.

"How does his place look if you been over his house?"

"He has a peach colored house. On the inside his mother has those Black leather couches with that Black and Burgundy rug on the carpet with that panther in the middle. She got a whole bunch of African Art and ceramic elephants everywhere. Shit we were fucking on his full size bed next to the dresser where he keeps the condoms. Matter of fact, bitch, why don't you count how many condoms he has. See if he has less than he had before." Lisa taunted.

Deidre opened the dresser and found only one condom. She wanted to cry but she still needed proof. Not Julani she thought, he couldn't be doing her like that. She had to make sure.

"What kind of condoms he used?"

"I don't remember the name brand but the package was black and gold. They were ribbed condoms because I felt them when we were fucking." Lisa replied.

Deidre was so furious that she hung up the phone in Lisa's face. She knew without a shadow of a doubt that Lisa was telling the truth. Then it made sense why Julani had unplugged the phone. She thought that was crazy because his mother might call. But he unplugged the phone so that if Lisa called he wouldn't hear the call. She sat on his bed mad as hell. She was so furious she didn't know what to do. She wanted to punch him in his lying mouth. All those times he was accusing her of shit was because he was doing shit she reasoned. Julani was still asleep totally unaware of the drama that he was in. She began to cry letting the tears fall profusely. Then she got up and walked into the bathroom. She couldn't let him see her cry. She loved that nigga and would have given him anything he wanted. How could he do this to me?

"Wake yo punk ass up, nigga!" She screamed while shaking him firmly.

"What the fuck, why are you waking me up baby I was having a good dream." Julani said startled and irritated.

"Were you dreaming about that bitch Lisa or were you dreaming about both of us?" Deidre fired back.

Julani woke totally out of his slumber after hearing the name Lisa. He wondered if he had said her name in his sleep. He wanted to play it by ear and see how much trouble he was in.

"Baby what are you talking about?" He played innocent.

"Now you don't know anyone named Lisa? The bitch you fucked the same day you fucked me. Around ten Wednesday night you and Jeff had a little company. She said that you both fucked on your bed."

"Aw baby, you can't believe everything you hear. People might say something because they're trying to break us up." Julani calmly replied. He was playing cool on the surface but there was emotional turmoil going on inside of him. He didn't know what to do but stay cool.

"Nah nigga, you can't wiggle out of this shit. She knew too much about you. She knew too much about your house." Deidre said with conviction.

"Oh, I remember Lisa, she was trying to get with me before you and I met. She probably was calling trying to hook back up. When she seen I had a girlfriend she decided to feed you a bunch of bullshit." He explained.

"So you knew her from seven or eight months ago? We have been dating for six and a half months. You brought her over your house back then." Deidre calmly asked.

"Yeah, and she been over my house only once. And that was almost a year ago. It was at least nine months ago." Julani confirmed.

"Uh huh, I caught yo ass in a bold face lie, nigga. She told me about the rug in the living room that your mother just bought. Remember we couldn't go to the beach that Saturday three weeks ago? You had to help your mother carry this new rug she wanted to buy with a panther on it. Your mother just got that rug three weeks ago and she knew all about it. You busted, just admit Julani yo ass is busted. She's been over your house at least within three weeks but she told me it was Wednesday night when I knew you wasn't with me."

Julani stood there stunned. He couldn't defend himself because she had him dead to rights. He was busted. Since he was sitting quietly that irritated Deidre even more.

"You ain't got shit to say now? You ain't shit Julani...yo ass ain't shit. Take me home, no matter of fact I'll have Marsha take me home. I'll use your phone and you don't have to see my ass again you rotten muthafucka." She yelled.

She called Marsha and told her to meet her on the corner of Atlantic and Market Street. She was so disgusted with Julani she didn't even want a ride from him. She packed her bags and walked out the door. Julani was devastated. He cried when she walked out the door. He had just lost his first love. And there was no one to blame but himself.

6
THE MONOGAMOUS SLUT

Julani still wanted to be with Deidre but she wasn't having it. She wouldn't accept his calls. She told her mother to tell him to stop calling. Deidre's mother liked Julani but if her daughter was through with him then she felt that he should leave her alone. Julani accepted the fact that he wasn't going to get Deidre back this time. He decided to move on. Since Lisa was the one that got him into this mess he figured he might as well hook up with her. He thought she looked good with a pretty face and a humongous booty. Like Jigga said 'he don't chase em' he replace him.' Julani considered. He wasn't going to skip a beat without Deidre in his life. Truthfully he was only lying to himself. His hurt was buried deep down within because he knew their break-up was entirely his fault.

But Lisa was the menu for the time being. She was different in several ways. Lisa had a street side that Deidre never possessed. Lisa would ditch school every now and then. She also smoked weed when she got a chance. And if you caught her on the wrong day she could curse like a sailor. Though she had all these faults, Lisa liked Julani very much.

"I ain't that stupid ass girl Deidre, you cheat on me and I'm gon' do more than break up with yo ass. I don't play that shit nigga." Lisa firmly stated.

"Nah baby that was a little mistake I made because I was digging you so much. I ain't really that type of nigga." Julani dismissed the accusation.

"Uh huh, I know this much Julani, as long as you straight with me I'm straight with you. If you want some pussy just say that but don't be trying to fuck all kinds of bitches on me." She persisted.

"I told you I ain't like that. Damn, I make one mistake and everybody labels me a no good nigga."

"I ain't saying all that, I'm just saying that I don't want any games. You love me right and I'll love you right."

So now that Lisa and Julani were a hot item he could now keep his mind off of Deidre. Since Lisa and Deidre were two different types of women there would definitely be things he would miss from Deidre. For instance Deidre brought out the inquisitive side of Julani. The side in him that wanted to know and learn things was what she inspired in him. She made him smarter and she made him want to be smarter. She was a true treasure with a beautiful spirit to go with it. Lisa on the other hand could show a mean streak that would bother Julani. She was also a loud mouth girl when she wanted to be. Lisa liked to have sex more than she liked to kiss. She wasn't into public displays of affection. She thought that was punk shit. But whenever Julani wanted some sex she was there to eagerly give it to him. They were both about to be seniors in high school.

It was the summer and they would spend a number of days together. They mostly had sex but every now and then they would do something recreational. Going to Six Flags Magic Mountain was one of their outings. They were having a good time together one particular day. Julani went to buy cotton candy from one of the vendors. On his way there he happened to notice Marsha, Deidre's best friend. His mind went blank because he knew that Marsha might tell Deidre that he was with another girl. Even if Deidre didn't want him anymore he still felt that she didn't need to know about who he was dating. Then he saw Deidre. Damn, he thought; because now Deidre seen him. She looked at him and you could tell that her eyes were about to water. She still hadn't gotten over him. He put his head down and tried to walk away.

"You don't know me anymore Julani; you can't even speak when you cheated on me?" Deidre emotionally asked.

"It ain't like that Deidre; it just ain't a good time to talk. I miss you like crazy but this isn't a good time to talk. Call me though!" Julani replied. Not giving her a chance to respond he quickly walked off.

He met up with Lisa back in the line of 'Batman the Ride'. Lisa smiled when she saw him cutting through the line to get to her.

"Julani we should get on the Riddler's Revenge after we get off of this one." Lisa excitedly suggested.

"Yeah that's cool!"

He was trying to conceal his pain the best he could but he was finding it extremely difficult. They rode on Batman the Ride together and screamed until their lungs fell out. They had so much fun on the ride they continued laughing while they exited the ride. For a brief moment Julani had forgotten about all his woes.

When they made the turn exiting the roller coaster perimeter Marsha, Deidre and three of their friends were standing outside looking right at them. Julani was devastated. He could see Marsha asking Deidre 'You want to beat that bitch's ass?" Deidre shook her head giving them both a pass. Julani was relieved but sad at the same time. He quickly rushed over to the Riddler's Revenge line.

"Why were you all up in that bitch's face at the Batman Ride?" Lisa asked.

"Nah, I just thought I knew her from somewhere that's all."

"I was going to see if yo punk ass was about to lie. That was that bitch Deidre and her homegirls. I seen that picture you have of both of you. As many times I been over your house you should have known that I've seen it. You probably still want to fuck with her." She retorted.

Her eyes were filled up with water. She hopelessly tried to hold back her tears. All she could do was wipe the lone tear that fell from her face as quickly as possible. Then she socked him in his arm.

"Baby, we're having a good time, we don't have to spoil it because we seen Deidre." Julani calmly suggested.

"It ain't that we seen Deidre it's the fact that you feel you gotta lie. If you had told me the truth I wouldn't have had an issue. And if that bitch wasn't with all her friends I would have went off on her." Lisa snapped.

Julani began looking around at the other Magic Mountain patrons. Suddenly embarrassed he tried to diffuse the situation.

"Baby, I'm sorry for lying I just didn't want any trouble. I wanted this to be a good day for both of us."

"Don't let that shit happen again Julani!" She replied.

Julani walked behind her and put his arms around her neck. He began grinding against her booty. He gently started kissing her neck.

"I promise baby, it won't happen again." He whispered.

They rode on two more rides then decided to leave. Luckily they didn't see Deidre or her friends for the rest of the night. They were able to get a hotel room through a friend. They went back to the hotel and relaxed. Lisa got out of her clothes. She was walking around the room in a thong and a half shirt with no bra. She had Julani wanting to jump all over her. She knew how to keep his mind off of Deidre. He had her stand right in front him while he played with her booty. She would shake her ass while he kissed her ass cheeks. Then he stood up and dropped his pants to the floor. He turned Lisa around and made her put her hands on the bed. While she bent over he opened her ass cheeks and penetrated.

"Ooh like that Lani baby, like that!" She moaned.

Once again he began riding her like she was a thoroughbred in the Kentucky derby. He was getting more excited while her ass bounced against his pelvis. Her booty was just bouncing away until he dug his fingers into her ass cheeks.

"I love you so much Lani, give it to me hard." She pleaded.

Julani began sweating profusely on his forehead. He could feel it all over that it was about that time. Whenever she felt him about to cum she would grab his leg because she knew he liked it that way. Then all of a sudden he began to feel it all over his body. As though it was perfectly timed he released. He fell on her back while she remained bent over. They had developed their sexual routine.

"That's it baby, I made you feel good?" She whispered while still caressing his leg.

Julani had cum but he was still inside of her. He lied on top of her as though he was trying to regain his strength. She continued

47

rubbing his leg as a gesture to calm him down. It took him a moment to reply from shortness of breath.

"Uh huh baby, you made me feel real good."

He finally pulled out still feeling dizzy from the orgasm. Once he stood up she eagerly walked towards the bathroom. He followed right behind her. They took a hot shower together then fell on the King sized bed.

They playfully argued over the remote control. Lisa was content with being stubborn about the television. Julani played with her for a moment then eventually fell into a deep sleep. Later that night Lisa turned on the porno station. She was attempting to get more attention from him. That was Lisa's way of getting attention from her man. She always proposed sex. But Julani had had his nut so he wasn't that excited. He saw that it was nothing but white pornos after waking up from his slumber then fell back into a deep sleep moments later. That hinted to Lisa that she needed to do the same. They would have to leave the room by eleven and it was already two in the morning.

That following day Julani made it home that morning to be greeted by his mother at the door.

"How are you doing baby; that nice pretty little girl Deidre called you? I told her you were out but she will probably be calling again soon." His mother smiled

"What time did she call mama?" Julani asked. He tried to conceal his eagerness.

"Around ten this morning. She told me she seen you at Magic Mountain with that fast tale girl Lisa. What happened between you and Deidre? She is a good girl with manners and aspirations. Why did you settle for that ghettofied Lisa when you had such a precious girl like Deidre?"

"We just couldn't spend the time together, that's all." He sadly replied.

"Well she sounds like she still loves you. Boy don't be any fool and pass her up. I seen that other girl with the big butt and nice shape. Julani those kinds of girls come a dime a dozen. I know you are having sex now because I seen the condoms in your drawer but be careful. It is a lot of fast tale girls that will give you nothing but problems. Once they have sex with you they play these games on men. Some have babies just to keep you around. Don't let them take away your future."

"I know but what if the girl you love doesn't want you. You eventually have to move on don't you?"

"If you're talking about Deidre, you are more naïve than I thought. That girl still wants you; I can hear it in her voice. Besides, you need to be with someone special. Deidre is special! Don't become a monogamous slut." Mama scolded.

"What's a monogamous slut?" Julani looked puzzled.

"A woman or a *man* that sleeps with every person they date. If they are dating you at the time then they are having sex with you. These people go from relationship to relationship having sex but can't find love. They find plenty of sex but not that much love."

"How can you find love when sex is all around you?" He asked.

"Boy you have found love! Deidre is a girl you can have something with. Lisa already got weed lips and she is just a senior in high school. She will probably be burnt out by the time she is twenty five."

"How do you know what burnt out is Mama?" Julani teased.

"I heard you and Jeffrey in the room talking. Plus a lot of that slang you use today has been used before when I was growing up. They just changed things around. But she is moving too fast for you. She is not going in the same direction that you are."

"Well I'm going to call Deidre right now. I'll talk to you later mama!"

"Okay Julani, but remember you can't be a monogamous slut. Pick a good girl and stick with her. Deidre is a good one." She yelled after him.

"Okay mama!"

He eagerly went into the room and called up Deidre. He was a little afraid because her mother told him not to call anymore. The phone rang three times before someone answered.

"Hello?"

49

"Hello, can I speak to Deidre?"

"This is me Julani; I thought this was your mother calling back."

"My mother told me you both talked."

"Yeah, your mother has always been cool." She replied.

"So what's up?" Julani impatiently asked.

"I want to see you that's all!"

"When?"

"How about tomorrow around noon but you are going to have to pick me up." She replied

"That isn't a problem Deidre and you know that."

"Where will your little girlfriend be? You know we could have beaten her down at Magic Mountain?" Deidre flared up.

"I know, I was able to read Marsha's lips."

"That's the same girl that you cheated on me with, huh?"

"Why we got to get all into that. You know that I love you. You are my heart I just made a stupid mistake. If you give me a chance I will never make that mistake again. I promise." Julani pleaded.

"I'll see, I'll see."

Julani and Deidre got off the phone with plans for the very next day. But Julani had to explain why he wasn't going to be able to spend time with Lisa tomorrow. She was already suspicious so he had to come up with a lie that would really make her believe him. If she got any hint that he was up to something she would blow up. He took a deep breath. He picked the phone up from off the base and dialed slowly. The phone rang once. The phone rang twice. Right before the third ring someone picked up the phone.

"Hello?"

"Hello, this is Julani can I speak to Lisa?"

Someone yelled to Lisa that Julani was on the phone. It sounded like Lisa's younger sister Lena. Julani heard someone put the phone down. Then he heard the phone pick up from somewhere else.

"I got it, you can hang up now." Lisa yelled.

Julani didn't say anything until he heard the other phone hang up.

"Hello Lani baby what's going on?"

"Nothing, what are you into?"

"I just finished washing dishes. It was my night in the kitchen."

"What are you doing tomorrow?" He went straight to the point.

"Why, what do you want to do?"

"Jeff and I were going up to the car expo to pick up some parts for our car around noon. You want to go?"

"Ya'll are going to be messing with cars all day? I can't do that all day I'll be bored." She pouted.

"Come on now it'll be a little fun." Julani falsely persuaded.

"Nah, plus you gon' be with that nigga Jeff. That pretty ass nigga can get on my nerves. What time do you plan on getting back?" Lisa asked, sounding slightly irritated.

"Around five you want to do something after that? We can go to the movies or something when I make it home." He offered.

"Yeah, that'll be cool. Just call me when you get back." Lisa sounded relieved.

"Alright I'll talk to you later?" He replied.

"Okay baby I'll see you tomorrow night."

Julani had eased his way out of a tough situation. He knew that she didn't really care for Jeff. And he also knew that she would not be interested in a car expo. It worked out just as he had planned.

7
ALL MEN ARE DOGS!

Julani was at Deidre's house at eleven thirty in the morning. He couldn't wait to see her. He sat in his car for about ten minutes meditating and praying. How was he going to face her after the last crazy incident? His confidence had become stronger but it was weak when it came to Deidre. He wasn't going to let a big booty come between him and his sweetheart. All these things were going through his head. His thoughts were suddenly interrupted by a feminine voice from outside.

"Julani, why are you sitting in the car, come inside?" Deidre yelled from inside the house.

He made sure everything was looking nice and clean before he got out the car. He was more nervous than a hooker in church. She waited for him to get to the door then opened the door. He tried to kiss her on the lips but she made sure that he only kissed her cheek. She told him to take a seat while she went into the other room.

"I would offer you something to drink but we are about to leave. If it's alright I would like to go back to your house?" Deidre asked from her bedroom.

"Yeah, sure we can go back to my house. My mother is not there today because her and my aunt drove down to San Diego." He nervously replied.

"I thought your mother and aunt don't get along?"

"They go back and forth and off and on. One minute they are sharing everything and the next minute they don't have anything to say to each other. I can't keep up with their feuds so I just leave it alone." He smirked.

That subject sort of lightened up the atmosphere. He started to relax a little more.

"Yeah I know that's right. You want to go to the park by your house and get some fresh air so we can talk." Deidre asked.

"Yeah, I'm with it."

"What did your mother drive down to San Diego for? What's out there?"

"They have some big outdoor swap meet her and my aunt likes to go to. You know those elephants in my house she buys some of them from that place."

"Oh, okay I heard about that swap meet or flea market whatever you want to call it." She replied while walking out the bedroom.

"Yeah, I went a few times with her. But since I was coming to see you I told her that I didn't want to go." He explained. When he seen her come out the room he was stunned by her beauty. He had a newfound respect for the way she carried herself. Her elegance he had once taken for granted was captivating after dealing with Lisa in recent times.

They jumped into his car that he had slowly been fixing up to look nice. He put a nice paint on his car and also a sound system. Deidre complimented what he had done to his car before they drove off. They drove off with his system playing full blast.

"So we are going to talk when we get to the park?" Julani asked. He turned down the music to be heard.

"No I've changed my mind, let's just go to your place and relax. We can watch a little television or whatever."

Julani was hoping for the whatever. When they pulled up to his house he really got to see what she was wearing. Deidre always knew how to dress with class. Even if it was hot as hell she could dress light and still look classy. She knew how to look sexy without looking like a slut. Since Julani was somewhat of a mama's boy he liked women that carried themselves like his mother. They didn't have to necessarily look like his mother but be conservative like his mother. Deidre was wearing loose beige shorts with a matching tank top and some wedges sandals. Her legs were shining from body oil or baby oil. Her toenails and fingernails were a matching light burgundy that went good with her complexion. She was simply awesome.

The thing about Deidre was that she didn't act stuck up. She was the most down to earth girl considering how attractive she was. Her confidence never could be mistaken for arrogance. When she turned a guy down she made him still feel good about it. He would be disappointed but she would thank him for the compliment anyway. How could a man disrespect a woman like that? Julani knew he had lost someone of value way before his mother told him. Now she was at his house once again. He was going to treat her with the utmost respect.

"Why are you acting all shy, damn Julani you met a girl with a booty bigger than mine so now I don't turn you on?" Deidre taunted.

"Nah, I just thought you wanted to talk. I was trying to be respectful Deidre that's all." He explained.

"You can be respectful and still give me some attention." She commented. She rolled her eyes at him in a playful way. His heart fluttered.

He moved closer to Deidre. She sat there as though she was inviting him to do whatever he wanted. He began kissing her on her neck and her chest. He started kissing her on her face until he kissed her on the lips. She kissed him back but wouldn't allow him to French kiss her. Though he was a little frustrated he continued on other parts of her body. He softly touched her breast and slipped his hands under her tank top. He began sucking on her small beautiful breast.

Julani helped her take off her tank top while he moved down to her belly button. While he was licking and kissing her stomach he unbuttoned her shorts. She helped him. His excitement intensified once he realized that she had intentions on being sexual. He helped her slip out of her shorts over her wedges sandals. While she stood butt naked with sandals on he eased her into his bedroom. He quickly took off his clothes and laid her on the bed. Her intoxicating aroma made him slide his tongue all over her body. She grabbed his head while his tongue explored her clitoris. He moved his mouth from her vagina all the way to her neck with the roll of his tongue. She shuttered in ecstasy. Once he climbed on top of her he began to gently touch sensitive parts of her anatomy with his fingers. She planted her fingernails into his back and drew his body closer. He gracefully slid between her legs.

"You got a condom?" She quickly asked.

She never asked Julani for a condom before because she took birth control pills. She always trusted him but never wanted to get pregnant at a young age. Now he could see that she didn't trust him anymore. He nodded his head and went into the dresser drawer to pull one out. He put the condom on quickly and penetrated before she changed her mind altogether. He began going slow and hard. She grabbed his ass trying to help him push into her more. She gave a resounding shriek of pleasure. He tried to push harder with long slow strokes. The sensual perspiration covered her entire body. They passionately intertwined allowing their lust to dictate their rhythmic movements. Her body trembled as she gave an even louder shriek than before.

Her cries indicated to Julani that she had cum. Now he bent her over and started doing it to her doggy style. Her low tone moans went in rhythm with each thrust coming from Julani. Then without expecting it so soon he exploded. The excitement had gotten the best of him. He released into the condom as she turned her head to look at him. She could feel the change. She could connect with his seductive climax.

"I almost forgot how good you make me feel." Deidre commented.

"I will never forget how good you make me feel." Julani replied. He gazed into her eyes as though he was in love all over again. Now they had both collapsed on the bed. They lied on top of the comforter facing one another.

"Let's cuddle for a little while if that's okay with you." She asked.

"Yeah, baby it's okay. Are we going to talk about us hooking up again?"

"We are hooking up right now. We just got through having sex didn't we?" Deidre suggested. Her tone was clearly sarcastic.

"Yeah, but you know what I mean, relationship wise?" He persisted.

"I told you we would see. Now relax and stop messing up the mood. Let us be happy that we are together right now." She calmly replied. Julani noted that she still hadn't given him an answer.

Julani would have to settle for that right now. He was thankful that she came by in the first place. He honestly thought that he wasn't going to see her again. She held him tight as if she was going to lose him at any given second. All it did was make Julani reminisce about his first love. She was the first woman that he had a serious love affair where there was mutual interest. No other woman would ever replace that unless the woman became his wife. He had done her wrong and knew that if given another chance he would never mess her over again.

"So what about your girlfriend Lisa?" Deidre interrupted his thoughts.

"Why are you bringing her up when you said that it was messing up the mood? Let's not talk about her. Let's just enjoy the moment and have a good time." Julani pleaded.

"Well we have been lying here for some time now and I am getting restless." She said getting up from the bed.

"You want to get in the shower. That is something that we always liked to do." He followed suit.

"You run the water and I will get in after you. Does your mother still have her shower caps in her bathroom?"

"Yeah, you remember where they are?"

"If they are in the same place, I should find them. But start the shower." She rushed him on.

"Alright!"

Julani ran into the bathroom and started running the shower. She stayed in the bedroom a little while after he got in the shower. He started worrying about ten minutes in and stepped out to call her.

"DEIDRE, DEIDRE ARE YOU GETTING IN OR WHAT?"

"Here I come; I was in your kitchen getting me something to drink."

"For ten minutes?" Julani replied. He sounded very condescending. She pretended to not notice his tone.

"No I was reading that Black History calendar your mother has in the kitchen and I got carried away. Quit tripping I am in here now."

She sure was Julani thought. He didn't have to give it a second thought. If he could get her to have sex in the shower it would be a wonderful thing. But she wasn't as affectionate as she was before. She allowed him to soap her body up and down like usual; however, she was still avoiding his advances when it came to kissing. That bothered him deep down in his soul. He knew that even if they did get back together it would never be the same. All of the innocence of their relationship was gone. He had hurt her and it showed. He tried to be optimistic and consider that she had to get comfortable with him again. On the other hand she was comfortable enough to have sex with him but not kiss? See that scenario was acceptable from Lisa but not from Deidre.

Lisa displayed her affection for her man through sex. She gave him sex whenever he wanted because she thought that was what would make him happy. Lisa didn't know any better because there wasn't a man significant enough in her life to show her different. Deidre had her father in her life. She saw how a man and a woman interacted when they were in love. She knew that there was more to pleasing a man than just giving him sex. Most women think that they know but their actions show something entirely different. Julani was only seventeen years old and could tell the difference. Within the last year he had been in a relationship with both kinds of women. This disturbed him because he wanted the old Deidre back. What bothered him even more was the fact that he was probably the reason she changed.

Once Deidre got out the shower she was ready to go home. He tried to prolong her stay but she seemed adamant.

"You don't have to go so soon we have a few more hours to hang out." Julani pleaded.

"I need to get home Julani, it is some things that I need to do today." She dismissed him.

"Are you sure you can't stay a little while longer. Besides, we never got to talk about you and me hooking back up in a relationship. Look Deidre I'm not going to fuck with that girl again. I'll be true to you and only you."

"I told you we would see, dang Julani quit acting desperate." She sneered.

Once she said those harsh words his ego stopped him from pushing the issue. He would be damned if he looked desperate. He wanted her bad but not at the cost of his pride. He quickly got dressed and escorted her out the door. Deidre knew attacking his pride would kill the issue. She had been with him long enough to know what buttons to push. They were both silent as they got inside his car. He sped off in his car and took her directly home. They pulled up in front of her house and he parked the car.

"At least tell me when will I see you again?" Julani asked. She could sense the pessimism in his voice.

"I don't know Julani; if it wasn't for my father I would think that all men are dogs." Deidre admitted.

"You think that all men are dogs because I made a mistake?" He said incredulously.

"You made two mistakes, because just as much as I was your girl when you fucked Lisa, she is your girl now and you had sex with me. How can you expect me to think you have changed when you had sex with me while you are dating her? You can't be trusted."

"I made a mistake with her but I didn't make a mistake with you. I love you and truly want to be with you. It was a moment of lust with her Deidre you gotta believe me."

"I believe you loved me but I also believe that you don't know how to love someone. Your selfishness is what keeps you from truly loving someone."

"Deidre I am only seventeen, people make mistakes when they are young."

"But people learn from their mistakes after they make them. Look Julani I have to go."

She didn't give him a chance to respond. She jumped out the car before he could say another word.

She turned her back on him and walked into the house. He sat in his car stunned for a minute. He knew that she was right he just didn't know how to handle it. He finally started his car and drove off. Little did he know that there was another conversation going on while he was driving home.

"Hello?"

"Hello, can I speak to Lisa."

"This is Lisa, who is this?"

"This is Deidre, remember me, I was dating Julani right before you were?"

"Yeah, I know who you are but how did you get my number? Bitch don't be calling here starting shit."

"Look girl I am not calling to start any trouble. I just wanted to let you know that your man is trifling. I just got through fucking him about an hour ago. I stole your number off of the caller ID. I figured your number was different because of the area code. I fucked him one last time for payback for when you fucked him." Deidre taunted.

"Bitch I didn't know he had a woman when I fucked him." Lisa fired back.

"Yeah but you were quick to throw it in my face when you found out he had a one. I don't want him Lisa, because he can't be trusted. If I wanted him I could have him. If you don't believe me I can call him on the three-way right now? I called you to tell you that you are dealing with a nigga that don't really want you and girl you are better than that."

"Why are you so concerned and what do you care if he wants me or not?"

"Because I don't think any woman should feel the way I felt when he did me like that. And woman-to-woman I don't have a problem with you my problem is with him. But you can't say I didn't warn you."

Lisa hung up the phone in her face. She ran into the room to cry. Everything Deidre told her she knew was true. All she was to Julani was a rebound and she knew it. She always knew it.

8
IT'S A TIME TO LOVE AND A TIME TO HATE

"You are a sorry muthafucka Julani! You had that bitch over your house when you said you and Jeff were going to some Auto convention. How many other bitches have you fucked since we've been together?" Lisa lashed out.

"Just Deidre and only Deidre." Julani calmly replied.

"So you admit doing that shit. Nigga I should have my cousins come and whip yo ass. How could you do me like that? We had a good thing going and you just fucked it up." Lisa said as tears began to fall from her face.

"I should have told you that I wasn't over Deidre. I'm sorry that I hurt you like that but it wasn't intentional."

"Whatever nigga you ain't shit."

"What we had wasn't love anyway Lisa. To tell the truth I had sex with you before we even kissed. You were more into sex than you were into affection. How is somebody going to fall in love with a woman like that?"

"Oh so now it's my fault that you cheated?"

"No it's my fault but you sure didn't give me affection like you gave me sex. Sometimes you act like a man as if sex is nothing but physical to you. I can't explain it but I wanted more than just sex from you."

"What about the times we had together like Magic Mountain and stuff?" Lisa began crying.

"I had a good time with you at Magic Mountain but when I seen Deidre some feelings came back to the surface." Julani admitted.

Lisa looked at Julani with piercing eyes. If her eyes were glass he would have been cut to pieces. She knew it was some truth to what he said but that is how she was introduced to sex. Her last boyfriend was a thug and he hardly kissed but he loved to have sex.

The thing that bothered her more than anything was that she still wanted Julani. Even after he cheated on her and gave her such harsh truth.

"Deidre and I became friends' way before we became lovers. You and I had sex then tried to do something after I broke up with Deidre. It just wasn't the same." Julani interrupted her thoughts.

Lisa didn't respond she just pondered on what he said. Her pride was hurt and her ego was shattered. She felt like Julani just called her a slut. She knew he didn't but it had the same effect as if he did. She tried desperately to control her anger but to no avail.

"I hate yo muthafuckin ass. I hope I never see you again for the rest of my life. Just leave me the fuck alone." She screamed. Lisa turned from him and ran into the house.

Julani walked back to his car feeling sad. He knew that he had wronged Lisa but he felt that he had to tell her the truth. He learned a lesson that weekend. He promised himself that he would never cheat on any woman that he was dating. It was too much drama first of all. Second of all too many people got hurt and he didn't like looking like a dirty dog. Julani felt that he was a good guy that made a mistake. But now he knew two women that didn't think he was a nice guy. This would have to be a painful lesson that would teach him to be better. His best friend Jeff probably could be a player but it wasn't in him to be that way. Julani went home and stayed in his room for the rest of the day.

For weeks he stayed to himself. He would hang out with Jeff but that was really about it. Bruce was preoccupied because he had gotten Terri pregnant. All his time was busy dealing with that. Julani was cool with it because sometimes he couldn't stand being around Bruce. He always thought Bruce was arrogant. Jeff would usually serve as a buffer between the two. Bruce appealed to Jeff's cocky side. Julani appealed to Jeff's down to earth respect for others side. Jeff always would tell Julani that he was a good dude. Jeff wanted to be like that, in fact, most times he was. But when it came to women Jeff could be ruthless. He didn't trust women so he treated them like he didn't. Jeff was what you would call a borderline misogynist. He loved women when it came down to sex but he never trusted them as friends.

"Shit women always say shit like I don't get along with other women. If they can't get along with their own sex and trust one another than a man doesn't stand a chance." Jeff vehemently repeated.

Julani respected Jeff's opinion but he disagreed. He believed that there were women out there that could be trusted. They just weren't an easy lot to find.

"Women might say that men can't be trusted. I cheated on Lisa and Deidre and got caught both times. That's two females that will always use me as an example of men being dogs."

"Yeah whatever nigga! You didn't do yo shit right. That's the reason why you got caught. How you gon' let a female roam around your house and you don't pay attention to what she's doing. Even if she just gave up the ass. Before that, you gave Lisa yo number when you should have only gotten hers. She was just a booty call and you let her have access to you like that." Jeff explained. He was good at espousing his player wisdom to Julani.

"She would have gotten it off her caller ID when I called anyway. I don't see the difference." Julani replied.

"All you had to do was tell Lisa that she shouldn't call because yo mother be tripping. That shit works all the time cause females always want to be cool with moms. Especially if they really like you." Jeff easily explained.

Julani chuckled to himself. Jeff always had an explanation for everything concerning the opposite sex. He shook his head knowing he didn't want to deal with the trouble.

"Men are supposed to have more than one woman. That is how it was in Africa. Women outnumber us seven to one. And that one nigga that wants to be faithful just gave me six more to add to my seven. A real player can fuck around and have fifty women all to himself." Jeff laughed.

"You crazy as hell dog, I just want one little winner. A girl with a cute face, big booty and some sense will be fine with me. As long as we can get along I'm fine."

"It ain't that simple. Anyway are you going with me to that dance on the West Side? It's gon' be a gang of hoes up there. Short, small, skinny, fat, tall, big booty, big titties and everything else will be there." Jeff spoke with enthusiasm.

"Yeah I plan on going. Whose car are we rolling in?" Julani asked.

"I was thinking that we roll in my car. Bruce stays on the West Side and I was going to pick him up on the way."

"Aw, that nigga going? I thought he was all in love with Terri? That nigga can get on my nerves sometimes." Julani protested.

"I know but since Terri is pregnant he's been looking for some new ass to hit. I told him about the party in passing and he said he wanted to roll. Remember when we didn't have cars and he would pick us up. He still got his mustang but he leaves it with Terri because she's pregnant. You ain't got to roll him in your car that is why I will roll mine."

"Fuck it, I ain't tripping. I wanted to ask you how you did on your SATs. I scored enough to get into Cal State Long Beach." Julani deliberately changed the subject.

"I don't know but I think that I scored enough too. I got to talk to my counselor next week."

"We're about to graduate and you still ain't taken care of that. You tripping big time." Julani warned.

"I know that is why I plan to meet with my guidance counselor to see where I stand. Don't worry homie I should be all right. I got a 2.8 GPA so we will see."

Friday night came quick for Julani. Now that he was a senior, school was a little more laid back for him. All he had to do was maintain his 3.2 GPA and he was going to Cal State Long Beach. He promised himself that he was going to have fun for his senior year. So he took classes that would insure that it was an easy year. He had already taken all the hard classes in his previous years. So he was hyped about going to this party. Jeff picked him up around nine-thirty. He put together this brown two-piece ensemble with matching K-Swiss. He walked out to Jeff's car feeling like a million bucks.

"Damn nigga, you look shitty sharp. I like the way you put that ensemble together. Especially with those tight ass K-Swiss." Jeff complimented him.

"Well I try, what can I say, I try!" He gloated.

They reach the West Side in about fifteen minutes. Bruce was already standing outside in his front yard when they pulled up. He must be eager Julani thought. Bruce was a heavyset guy but he knew how to wear clothes that complimented his size. He wore black jeans and a black San Francisco Giants jersey. He also had on K-Swiss but his were black. Bruce hopped in the backseat and they drove to the party.

When they got there it was a line as long as a block. They were letting ladies in first. Ladies got in free before ten-thirty. It was so many pretty women waiting outside that they all wanted to faint. There was a lot of competition there as well. High School girls wearing high heels and tight mini-skirts. Young women in tight jeans and blouses that showed cleavage appeared to be everywhere. Jeff, Julani and Bruce felt like they were kids in a candy store. They patiently waited to get inside because their view was excellent outside. But inside was where the music, food and drinks were. It was a little cold but not enough for the girls to stop wearing clothes that showed their assets. Sex and sexiness was in the air and all the men present were taking a deep breath.

After about thirty minutes of waiting outside they finally were able to get inside. They slowly walked in the dark room with the strobe lights flashing like they were the three musketeers. Julani posted up against the wall as Jeff and Bruce got something to drink. It was so many women to choose from that he relaxed so he could study the crowd. It was at least five women to one man. This party must have had some good promotion because every high school in Long Beach was present. Just like Julani imagined there were women of all shapes, sizes and colors. He looked around and a pretty caramel complexioned girl with a short bob hairstyle walked past him. As he inspected her she had all the equipment that he looked for physically. When she passed by she smiled at him. He smiled back but was touched by her smile. He was thinking about letting her pass by when he heard that Ginuwine song 'Differences'. He gently grabbed her arm.

"Would you like to dance?"

She nodded and they went to the dance floor. She was about five foot three with big legs and an ass that filled out her jeans. Her tight jeans hugged her bottom while she wore blue two-inch heals. She had a silk blouse that matched her shoes. She was small at the top but wide below her waist. As they got closer Julani felt himself getting stiff. He wasn't embarrassed in fact he pulled her closer. They were wrapped together tight as she laid her head on his chest. Julani got so comfortable that he decided to ease his hands down to her ass. She slowly pulled his hands back up. He secretly smiled trying to hold back from chuckling. He danced with her until the song was over. After that a fast song came on so he walked with her against the wall. He talked in her ear because the music was so loud.

"So what is your name?" He asked.

"Tammy" she smiled.

"My name is Julani. I seen you walking by and I had to talk to you."

"With all these girls in here you probably had to talk to a whole bunch of girls."

"Yeah it is a whole bunch of girls in here but I like you. What school do you go to?"

"I go to Milliken; I'm a junior this year. What school do you go to?"

"I go to Long Beach Poly. I'm a senior this year, next year I plan to go to Cal State Long Beach."

"That's cool, what are you going to major in when you get up there?"

"Communications and I am going to minor in Sociology. What do you plan to do after you leave Milliken?"

"I'm thinking about being a nurse. I want to become an RN but I haven't decided what college I want to go to."

"So where is your boyfriend at because as fine as you are I know that you are someone's woman?"

"Nah, I just broke up with my boyfriend about three weeks ago. I can't stand that nigga though." She frowned

"Well that's good to know; what did he do to make you hate him like that?" Julani replied. He didn't really care he just wanted to keep up the conversation.

"Being no-good, he was messing around with a girl I thought was my best friend. But I ain't tripping off of that anymore. Where is your girlfriend right now?"

"I don't have anyone either. I broke up with my girl about six months ago. But I don't hate her." He smiled.

"Yeah because you probably did something to her. You look like the player type." She teased.

"What's the player type? I'm a cool young positive brother why do you want to put that tag on me?" He chuckled.

"I don't know maybe I'm tripping!"

A girl equally as pretty walked across the room and waived to Tammy.

"Come on Tammy it's time to go. I have to be in the house in about thirty minutes."

"Okay here I come!" Tammy sadly replied.

"Let me get your number before you go?"

"Okay!" She eagerly agreed.

Julani pulled out his pen and pad so that she could write her number down.

"You probably gon' break my heart but you are cute as hell. Call me." She commented.

"Thank you. But don't prepare yourself to hate me because of your ex-boyfriend. Give yourself time to love and learn who I am. Your boyfriend was in the past baby I'm in your future."

She smiled and waved goodbye. Julani threw up the peace sign in his attempt to stay cool. Deep down he was excited because he knew that she liked him as much as he liked her. Jeff and Bruce walked over there to congratulate him on his pull.

"You pulled a little winner Lani. She got a big ole ass like you like. She didn't look bad in the face either. But nigga I done got four numbers so far and Bruce pulled two."

"I'm straight for the night. I got all the numbers I'm going to need."

"Nigga don't fall in love yet and you ain't even hit the skins. Give yourself some time to get to know if she is what you want. If you get a few numbers you can pick and choose which ones you really want." Jeff explained.

"The time is now and I am content with this female I just pulled."

Jeff threw up his hands in the air as a sign of surrender. He just didn't understand his best friend. Here he was still in high school trying to find the woman of his dreams. Julani smiled at Jeff because he knew what he was thinking without him saying a word. He vowed to himself that he wasn't going to get caught up in any kind of drama again. He was going to find someone he could chill with and make the best out of it. Now was the time for him to meet Tammy and see what she was all about.

9
PUNK BITCH

Julani and Tammy went on their first date that following Friday. His mother always taught him to never take a girl to the movies on a first date. He decided to take her to dinner and afterwards they would walk the Santa Monica Promenade. They went to Red Lobster to eat. Julani could tell that Tammy was extremely shy. She had an outgoing side but she was shy in the beginning. She was really impressed with the dinner date. It was her first dinner date with a guy. Julani had to go inside to meet her mother. Her mother was an older version of her. She was one of those mothers that looked just as good as her daughter. Julani could tell Tammy knew her mother looked good for her age. That might have made her a little insecure.

Tammy also had a younger brother and a stepfather. The stepfather shook Julani's hand but he could tell that the stepfather couldn't have cared less. He quickly went back into the den to watch television. Tammy's mother on the other hand wanted to meet him.

"So Julani, Tammy tells me you go to Long Beach Poly High School? What do you plan to do after school?" She inquired.

"I'm going to Long Beach State." Julani shyly replied.

"Oh, so do you know what you are taking up there?"

"Yeah, I'm going for Communications and I'm going to minor in Sociology."

"That's good; Tammy is going to be a RN like myself." She proudly replied.

"The night I met her she told me she wanted to be a nurse Mrs. Jones, that's good."

"No Julani, my last name is Avery but you can call me Pam. Where do you plan to go tonight?"

"Oh I'm sorry Pam but I wanted to take Tammy to Red Lobster."

Pam looked at Tammy and gave her a face of approval.

"Okay well you have a good time and make sure she is home by twelve." Pam rose from the table.

The first date was nice for both of them. After dinner they drove up to the promenade and walked around. He made her laugh a lot. He understood that Tammy didn't know how pretty she really was. Since her mother was the spotlight in the household she had an inferiority complex. Sometimes she would walk with her head down. But whenever Julani talked to her she looked him in his eyes. He thought that she was very intelligent. This was a change from Lisa. Lisa was street smart but that was about it. She was smart in many different subjects, which impressed Julani. She wasn't religious but she claimed to be non-denominational. He never chose a religion for himself he just wanted to believe in God. She wasn't as outgoing and charismatic as Deidre but that was also good. Her dressing was simple but pretty with a touch of sophistication.

On their first date she wore a jean mini-skirt. She had on navy blue heels and a navy blue blouse. It was attractive but conservative. Her mini-skirt came to her knees. When she sat in his car was the only time he got to see her thick thighs. Her thighs were nice and shiny as though she had put a gallon of baby oil on.

"Blue must be your favorite color, because when I met you, you were wearing blue?" Julani asked.

"I love blue; especially royal blue that is really my favorite color. I guess if I gangbanged I would be a Crip." She giggled.

"I guess so, but you make it look good whatever you wear."

"Thank you, but I like the way you dress also. You like those earth tone colors I see. You were wearing brown when I met you but now you are wearing beige. Those two guys that were with you that night are they your best friends?"

"You've seen me with those two other guys?" Julani asked. He was surprised she noticed Bruce and Jeff.

"Yeah, I seen when all three of you walked in."

"So you were scoping me once I walked in the door." Julani arrogantly smiled.

70

"I wouldn't say all that. But I did think you were cute. Answer this for me, why did you take me out to eat? I thought you were going to take me to the movies." She quickly changed the subject.

"You wanted to go to the movies?"

"No, I'm not saying that, it is just what I expected."

"My mother told me to never take a girl out on the first date to the movies. How can you get to know someone when you are both looking at a movie? You get to know someone while you are eating. You can also tell how a girl carries herself at the dinner table."

"So how did I do? Did I pass your dinner table test?"

"Well let me see, you didn't chew with your mouth open. You didn't talk while food was still in your mouth. I would say that you carried yourself like a lady should. What about me?"

"You have good manners also. It was a pleasure to share a meal with you Mr. Julani Jasper." She giggled.

They both laughed while walking back to the car. Julani could honestly say that he had a good time. He definitely wanted to see her again. He made sure she was at her porch by 11:45. He walked her to the door and they gave each other a soft kiss on the lips then said good night.

"I'll call you tomorrow; maybe we can get into something." Julani said. He had already begun walking towards his car.

"Okay, call me!" She replied.

Julani made it home from his date feeling good. He walked into his house and noticed his mother was still awake. While he grabbed grape juice out of the refrigerator he started singing En Vogue's 'Giving him something he can feel'. His mother laughed to herself.

"So who is she this time Julani? Boy I swear you fall in love too easy, I thought I raised you tougher than that." She chuckled.

"What makes you think that it is a girl, mama?"

"Shit, I damn sure hope it isn't a boy."

"You know what I mean. Who says that it's a relationship in the first place? I don't have a girlfriend right now." Julani laughed.

"You haven't been the same since that pretty girl Deidre was coming around. Whatever happened to her?"

Julani sat next to his mother on the living room couch. He didn't want to explain what he had done but he had to tell her something.

"We went our separate ways that's all. I went on a date with this girl named Tammy tonight."

"I knew it! Talking about '*who says that it's a relationship*'. I brought you in this world and raised you for almost eighteen years. So is she nice?" His mother teased.

"She seems real nice, I took her to Red Lobster for our first date and she was classy. She's not ghetto like that girl Lisa I used to date."

"So when will I meet her?"

"I don't know mama she's got to be special to meet *my mama*."

"I know that's right. Are you going to take her out again?"

"Yeah, hopefully we will get to go out again this weekend. We might go to the movies or something."

"Well treat her right Julani, but don't let her run over you. Women don't like men they can run over." She scolded.

"I know mama, when are you and Billy getting married?" He quickly changed the subject.

"I don't know, shit after your daddy I haven't been quick to jump back into a marriage. We are taking it slow. But you do like him though, huh?"

"Yeah, he's cool."

"Oh he's cool?

"Yeah, he seems real cool as long as he is treating you right."

"He's treating me good so far. It has been a good three years I must admit. But I like that we are taking it slow."

Julani finished his juice and got up from the couch.

"Good night mama, I'm tired. I'll see you in the morning."

"Okay, baby good night."

Julani was eager to go to sleep so he could wake up in the morning to call Tammy. He took off his clothes and collapsed on the bed. He hadn't felt this good about a girl since he was with Deidre.

The following morning he lingered around the house for a few hours. He didn't want to appear too eager so he waited until noon to call. Tammy had been waiting on his call all morning. Her family went on an outing without her because she was expecting to hear from Julani. He called her to take her to the movies. They could catch a matinee then go somewhere else afterwards. He told her he would be at her house at one in the afternoon. She was ready by twelve thirty.

They went to the movies and then walked Venice Beach. They were trying to get to know each other. Asking the important questions. They both were two young people with a promising future. They both were hoping that their futures could fit one another.

After about a month they considered themselves girlfriend and boyfriend. Now Julani felt it was time for them to make that big step. It was time to take the intimacy to another level. Julani was able to get her back to his house while his mother was at work.

"Julani are you sure you got condoms because I can't be getting pregnant." Tammy warned.

"Don't worry baby I got everything under control. I got a box of condoms in my top drawer." He smiled.

"A box of condoms? Why do you have all those condoms? How many girls are you messing with?" She complained.

"I haven't messed with anyone in a while. I told you that you are the only one I've been seeing. Why you keep asking me that?" Julani replied.

He had been getting the third degree as of lately about him seeing someone else. He thought she might have run into his old girlfriends or something. He hadn't given her a reason to be jealous as far as he could tell.

"I just need to know because I ain't no ho that you can just get into bed." Tammy fired back.

"I know baby I know." Julani calmly confirmed. It was more like surrender; he had been in this discussion with her before.

They made it back to his house and went into his bedroom. Julani could tell that she was nervous. He tried to make her as comfortable as possible. He offered her something to drink but she said no. She sat on the edge of his bed with all her clothes on acting stiff as a board. He tried to loosen her up with a few jokes. He always could make her laugh. But this time she gave short brief laughs. It was beginning to irritate Julani.

"Okay Tammy, if you don't want to do this we don't have to." Julani surrendered.

"No baby, that's not it I'm just a little nervous. But I don't want you to have an excuse to cheat on me." She replied.

"That's not a good reason to have sex with someone. I thought you wanted to do this because of how you felt about me?" Julani said.

"I do, but I only been with one other guy and that was a long time ago. I'm almost a virgin and I don't know if I'm ready for you. You probably have had plenty of experience."

"What makes you think I have had plenty of experience? I've had it more than once before but I am not that experienced." Julani lied.

He had only been with three women but it was a lot of sex with those three women. He was only seventeen but knew all of the freaky sexual positions. If Shay didn't show him something Lisa did. Deidre learned her moves from him. Just like Deidre he wanted to teach Tammy what he knew.

"Baby take off your clothes and let me show you how we can make love to one another." Julani smoothly said.

"Okay, Julani let's do this." She complied.

She slowly started taking off her clothes. She had on a beige silk blouse with a brown skirt. She had on thick three-inch beige leather heels with brown suede going across the front. Julani always liked the way his new girlfriend dressed. Now he was concentrating on her getting undressed. She was more conservative than Deidre even though Deidre was conservative most of the time. Now Tammy stood butt naked in front of him. His mouth was wide open as he looked at her flawless caramel figure. He quickly took off his clothes trying to remain cool. She smiled when he finally got undressed.

"Get your condoms Julani." She pleasantly suggested.

"Okay baby."

Julani went into his top drawer and pulled out his magnum condoms. He kept his eyes on her while ripping the condom package. Without hesitation he slid the lubricated condom on. He gently laid her on the bed. He began kissing on all parts of her body. She enjoyed the foreplay but was too nervous to participate. He began to orally explore the inner lips of her vagina with his tongue. Her pubic hairs were neatly cropped as though she shaved her hair regularly. She smelled of an aroma that intensified his lust for her. His mouth and her clitoris were entangled as one. She showed her satisfaction by grabbing his head and giving a low moan. Her first boyfriend had never made her feel like this.

He wanted to get her wet and horny. He wanted to build up her desire to make love. He gradually climbed on top of her. When they were face to face they began kissing slowly. He attempted to be patient by allowing the tip of his dick to rub against her clitoris. He put the tip of his manhood inside her vagina while continually grinding. He could feel her getting wetter as his loins began to spread inside her vaginal cavity. She let out a sharp silent shriek. He grabbed hold of her from the back to hold her still. She lied there breathless with her mouth wide open. She started to embrace the pleasure pain. Her perspiration began to intensify the aroma of her perfume. Julani sucked on her neck and chest. He was infatuated by the smell of the Vera Wang perfume she had taken from the top of her mother's drawer.

"Why don't you get on top?" Julani whispered.

"No baby lets keep doing it this way."

He wasn't prepared to stay in the same position. He wanted to explore every sexual position possible with Tammy. But now he had to satisfy her in the missionary position alone. He tried to spread her legs wider but they were locked in position. Then he felt her get into a rhythm that he decided to follow. She wrapped her arms around his back and pulled him closer. Suddenly she held him in place with both arms and feet. He could feel her getting hot.

"Oooh!" she moaned.

"Oh yeah." Julani added. He quickly pulled out and semen fell on the bedspread.

"Oh shit Julani the condom broke. Did you know that the condom was broken?"

"Nah, I didn't know." Julani was stunned.

All of a sudden Tammy started crying. She started crying so hard that Julani was in shock. He finally snapped out of it after a few seconds.

"Baby, what's wrong are you bleeding or are you hurt somewhere?" He pleaded.

"I can't get pregnant Julani, I can't get pregnant." She cried.

"Baby who said that you were pregnant. You don't even know if you're pregnant and you are crying over that?"

"I can't let my mother down. I can't disappoint her."

"Baby I didn't even cum inside of you. You don't know if you are pregnant. Stop jumping the gun." He calmly replied.

She fell back on the bed letting tears fall from her face. He felt like she was overreacting. He was so irritated about her outburst that he didn't consider that he might be a little insensitive. He let her lie there and cry herself to sleep. This was supposed to be a joyous occasion and she had turned it into an emotional roller coaster. Julani couldn't help but to think she was a punk bitch. Too fucking weak to have a normal healthy relationship. Maybe he was being insensitive he finally considered. After weighing both sides he had to say that she was definitely overreacting. Julani worried about his new relationship, maybe she was too weak. He liked strong women not women that cry every time something goes wrong. If she was that type which it appeared to be he was going to have his hands full.

10
MANIPULATION

It was summer time and Julani wanted to have fun. He just graduated from High School. He felt like a grown ass man. He had been dating his girlfriend Tammy now for nine months. It had been a decent relationship as long as he didn't make her cry. Julani was finding it easier and easier to make her cry. Especially now that he had graduated from High School she was paranoid about the college girls he might meet. Her crying was starting to drive him crazy. This was his first summer out of high school and he wanted to enjoy it before he started college. He was hoping that he could enjoy it with his girl but she kept making things difficult. He labeled her a drama queen.

The most recent incident was when they were in the mall. He took her to see a movie then they decided to walk through the mall. Everything was fine until they came across a Coogie dress in a women's clothing store. It was on display on the outside window.

"That would look good on me, huh?" Tammy asked.

"Anything would look good on you, baby." Julani replied.

"That style is different from what I would usually wear."

"Yeah, to tell the truth that is not your style. You are more conservative than that dress implies." He admitted.

"Oh what, I'm not grown enough for the dress?" She asked incredulously.

"Nah, I'm saying that it is not your style. It will still look good on you but you carry yourself different that's all I'm saying."

"Those girls at Long Beach State will probably being wearing clothes like that. Are you going to say that this dress is not their style?"

"I won't be saying anything because I will be thinking about my classes or you."

"Uh huh nigga you know you are going to compliment the shit out of those girls at Cal State. You probably will want to mess around with one of them too." She sneered.

"Baby, why do you have to go there? We were having a good time; don't spoil it with that kind of shit." Julani replied.

"Everything I say is bullshit to you. What I'm too young to say anything worth saying?" She fired back.

"I didn't say that. All I'm saying is that you don't have to worry about me messing with any other girls because I'm with you. So it is no need to bring that up."

"That's what your mouth says." She replied.

"That what my heart says too. Quit tripping!" He snapped.

"Oh so I'm tripping now? Do you need a mature woman that doesn't trip on you?" She screamed.

"I need a woman that will shut the fuck up." He blurted out.

Tammy looked at him with her puppy dog eyes. She then put her face in her hands and started crying. In the middle of the mall she was crying. Julani was embarrassed as hell at first. He started looking around to see if anyone is looking. He wiped the sweat from his brow then walked over to her.

"Baby, I'm sorry I didn't mean it like that. You don't have to worry about us breaking up. I don't want any other woman but you. Don't cry."

Julani couldn't believe that this was started over a Coogie Dress. His girlfriend was too sensitive for him. He knew it but he didn't know how to break it off with her. The number one reason he didn't want to break up with her was because she was steady sex for him. Julani wasn't like a lot of men that got a thrill off of the chase. In fact Julani hated the chase. He liked spending time with one girl and that was it. But now he was in a point in his life where sex had become addictive. If he didn't have sex every so often he would have withdrawals. Like when a drug addict doesn't have any drugs. When Tammy was mad at him the only way she could hurt him was deny him sex. Since he never cheated on her he would be in need after awhile. He would kiss her ass so that she would eventually give him some. She would usually put him on punishment for about a week or two. Julani knew that he would be on punishment for this argument. He tried to treat her nice while she gave him the silent treatment on the way home. Julani was hoping to get some after the date but he blew that. He decided to take Tammy straight home. She got out the car without even kissing him. He wasn't so much surprised as disappointed.

As he drove home he became angry. He couldn't believe they had gotten into another argument. He was supposed to have been getting off of punishment about an incident last week. He walked into his house infuriated. He began slamming doors and kicking walls. He grabbed something from the kitchen and slammed the cabinet door. Not knowing his mother was home he slammed the bedroom door and fell on the bed.

His mother followed closely behind him. She opened his bedroom door and stared at him. Leaning on the doorframe with her arms crossed she interrupted his depression.

"What the hell is wrong with you?" She firmly asked.

"Aw mama it's something personal"

"Tell me what it is and maybe I can help you with it. I bet you it has something to do with Tammy."

"Yeah, how did you know?"

"Because every time you come in here with your temper flaring it is because something Tammy has done. What happened this time?"

"She pissed me off again today. She started on this fit about a dress in the mall. I complimented her and everything. But she swore up and down that I would cheat on her when I go to Cal State Long Beach. I told her that she was too conservative for the dress but she would still looked good in it. I told her I just didn't think it was her style. She twisted it into meaning that I wanted to talk to older women."

"That girl is manipulating you with accusing of cheating all the time. Has she caught you cheating or have you cheated on her?"

"No mama I swear. We have been dating for nine months and I have been totally faithful."

"Yeah she got something on you though. That is the reason she keeps playing these silly games. She knows of a weakness that she can control you with."

"Not that I can think of. She doesn't have any control over me. I do what I want to do when I want to do it. She knows better than to try to boss me around." Julani said with confidence.

"Usually a woman uses something many men are weak about." His mother gave him a suspicious look.

"What's that?

"SEX! Does she deny you sex when she is mad at you?" She asked.

"All the time. That is the first thing that goes when she is hurt or crying."

"I thought I raised a strong independent young man. Not a man that can be easily manipulated by sex."

"What do you mean by that?"

"Julani, she gets mad at you easily so that she can keep you eating out of her hand. She knows that sex is your weakness so to keep you kissing her ass she gets mad easy so that she can deny you sex. When you are not mad at each other do you have sex a lot?"

"Aw mama we don't have to talk about how much we have sex."

"You are grown now Julani I expect that you are having sex regularly. So how many times, everyday, twice a week or what?"

"At least three times a week unless she is on her period." He admitted.

"Is she ever really mad at you when she is on her period?

"She might be a little irritable but come to think about it she never starts crying." He started considering his mother's logic.

"Yeah that is her way of keeping you on a leash. Son, do not allow any woman to control you with sex. Learn to be abstinent at times. She is going to keep playing those games until you learn how to control yourself."

Julani didn't respond to what his mother said. He was infuriated once he realized what Tammy was up to. It was only seven in the evening so he decided to drive over to Tammy's house.

He pulled up in front of the house wondering if he should knock on her door. He finally built up the courage to get out of his car. He sat on his car for a few seconds contemplating what he should do. He leapt from his car and walked towards the porch. His determination was relentless.

He rang the doorbell twice. Tammy' mother was the first to come to the door. She opened the door with an inviting smile.

"How are you Julani come on in?"

Julani walked in smiling. He politely spoke then entered the living room to take a seat. Tammy was in her room while everyone else was in the den watching television. Her mother knocked on the bedroom door and told Tammy that Julani was waiting in the living room for her. Tammy jumped out of her bed and walked into the living room with a perplexed look on her face.

"What are you doing here Julani, I wasn't expecting you?"

"I know but I needed to talk to you."

"It couldn't wait until tomorrow?"

"Nah, matter of fact why don't you grab your coat so that we can go outside."

"You can't talk to me inside the house? There is no one in the living room." She complained.

Control the environment and you can control the direction of the conversation Julani thought.

"No let's go outside. You got the taste for some McDonald's French Fries?"

"I always got the taste for some McDonald's French Fries." She smiled.

She loved when Julani was trying to make up to her. She was eager to see what he had in store for her.

"Go and grab your coat and meet me outside." He replied.

She ran in the room to get her coat. While coming out of the room she hollered to her mother that she was going to McDonald's with Julani. Julani was already waiting in the car with the engine running before she came outside. She eagerly jumped into his car to get her French Fries.

"Are you getting me some fries to make up for what you said earlier today?" She asked.

"No, but I did want to talk to you about what happened earlier today."

"You want to apologize but you always say you're sorry Julani; then you do something else to hurt me." She commented.

"Who said I was apologizing? I wanted to get something off my chest not apologize."

"Oh so you got something to get off your chest after you told me to shut the fuck up?"

"Yeah maybe I didn't handle the situation in the best of manners but you are the one that provoked it." He replied.

"How did I provoke you to curse at me?" She asked incredulously.

"You provoked me to…Hold on, let me get two orders of fries and two regular sized Orange Hi-Cs…no that will be all, thank you.

Julani waited until he paid for the food and picked it up. He gave her a box of fries and a drink then drove off.

"You provoked me because of you constantly accusing me of wanting to date other women. I haven't given you any reason not to trust me yet you act like you don't trust me all the time. If you don't trust me why are you with me?"

"Because I love you Julani. I'm just worried about you cheating on me because you are going to college. When you go to Cal State all kinds of girls are going to be after you and I don't know if you can handle it."

"If I can handle it? You are tripping! All I know is that I can make you cry off of the smallest things and it is starting to get on my nerves. No to tell the truth it has gotten on my last nerve." He retorted.

"So what are you trying to say?"

"I'm saying that maybe we should see other people. We don't have anything in common but sex and it seems like you are using that against me."

"How am I using it against you?"

"You always get upset off of the smallest things when you know I want to do something. You didn't think I noticed your little pattern huh?"

"Okay, I admit that I don't want to do it as much as you do. But that isn't a reason to break up with someone."

"Yeah it is! This whole relationship is based upon you trying to manipulate everything. At first I thought it was because you were real sensitive like that time we first had sex. But then I thought about it you are only sensitive when it fits your needs." He lashed at her.

"Where are you getting this shit from? Jeff and Bruce are putting some bullshit in your head."

"No don't try to use that be a leader not a follower bullshit. What about that time I wanted to go to the Nas concert with Jeff and Bruce. You made me feel guilty about going without you so I didn't go. What about when we were supposed to go to Magic Mountain but you didn't want get on any rides. So you cancelled at the last minute and made me feel bad about wanting to go. You even cancelled on my high school picnic and made me feel bad for going without you."

"It wasn't even like that!" Tammy started crying.

He couldn't control his anger when he seen her trying to manipulate him again. That was how he felt at the time. He looked her dead in her face.

"Get the fuck out of my car. I need to go home because yo ass is fired." He snarled at her.

She jumped out the car still crying. Julani drove off glancing through his rearview. He was able to tell that she wasn't crying by now. She stared at his car driving away then walked in the house. She might have been hurt but she wasn't crying. He was still amazed at how she was able to turn it on and off. He couldn't knock her game but he couldn't be a fool behind it either.

11
STANKIN ASS

Julani basically stayed single for most of his college career. He would date every now and then. Maybe he would meet a study partner and they would take it a step further than study. Or he might go to a University event and link up with someone for a short time. He was too busy in his life to really commit himself. He always was able to keep the women he dealt with at a distance. His excuse was that he was working and going to school. Some girls would cling on because they knew that Julani had a promising future. Then there were the ones that were just weak for him. He didn't have to be anyone's boyfriend, just spend some time and show a little attention and they were ready for sex.

That was when it dawned on Julani that he could be dead broke and pussy could fall in his lap. As for money that was a little harder to obtain than sex. If he was at the right place at the right time he could pull a girl that would be willing to fuck. It made him laugh because he remembered this comedian saying that if pussy were on the stock market it would plummet. He felt himself growing up.

Cheap sex was easy to come by for Julani during his college years. He was handsome, athletic, and ambitious and focused which were good ingredients for many women. He had everything that he could want and he didn't have to live in the dorms. In fact he and Jeff were about to get an apartment near the University. While he was enjoying the good single life Julani noticed a pretty woman smiling at him. Not an average pretty but a bombshell pretty. He was joking around between classes with Jeff when he noticed her stare. He had to double take because he wasn't sure if she was staring at him or Jeff. She smiled again but this time she waved. He'd seen her around the campus. She had smooth light caramel skin. She also had thick lips with a knockout smile. Her hair went

84

down to her shoulders, which she seemed to always keep done. She had light brown eyes and a very nice shape. She was petite with a little bubble butt but also top heavy. Her frame was small for her to be so voluptuous. She knew how to wear the clothes that complimented her sexy frame.

When she waved Julani pointed towards himself to see if he was whom she was referring. She nodded as if he was acting silly. He knew all the guys were trying to holler at her. If he wasn't mistaken she was the number one candidate for homecoming queen. Her pictures were all over the place. That was when it dawned on him that she must have wanted him for something concerning the Homecoming event. He walked over to greet her thinking suspiciously.

"How are you doing, I thought you were referring to my homeboy?" Julani smiled while shaking her hand.

"No I was referring to you Julani. My name is Melissa."

"How did you know my name, Melissa?"

"I asked around and people that knew you told me everything about you."

"People should mind their own business. But it is still nice to meet you. How can I help you?" He charmingly replied.

"I just wanted to talk to you. I think you are so cute. I finally built up the courage to talk to you."

"Thank you, you are very beautiful yourself."

"That is so sweet. To be honest with you I don't usually date dark skin guys but I had to talk to you."

Julani felt a little uncomfortable after she said that. What the fuck is that suppose to mean she doesn't date dark skin guys? Are we some fucking plague or something? I guess I am supposed to feel privileged because she wants to date me. While Julani was thinking these things she must have felt the tension during the silence.

"I don't mean for you to take it the wrong way it is just something I have never done. I was hoping to break that bad habit with you." She smiled.

Julani smiled.

"I hope you are not one of those black people that are color struck. Believing that the lighter you are the better. Because black is beautiful in all its shades." Julani explained.

"That is so true Julani I just was telling you about my past relationships. Trust me I'm not color struck. So you are majoring in Communication and Sociology huh?" Melissa quickly changed the subject.

"Yeah, I want to get into broadcasting. Maybe work behind the camera at a television station or something. Or I can also get into being a Probation officer. Both are things that I am into but whomever you asked about me knows a lot. Was it my homeboy Jeff?"

"No it was a few people including some girls that liked you as much as I do. I did a real good investigation before I waved at you." She smiled.

Julani looked up and seen Jeff and a couple of college buddies admiring the girl he had pulled.

"Those are your closest homeboys over there huh? Especially that guy Jeff, Mr. Player-Player." She giggled.

"Yeah, Jeff and I are real tight as for everyone else I met them up here. If you are free maybe we can go out sometime this weekend?"

"Yeah that will be nice. Next weekend I will be busy for Homecoming. So we can spend some time together this weekend." She replied.

"Let me get your phone number and I will call you."

"Okay!"

As she was writing her number down Julani looked over at his homeboys. They looked more excited than he was. He was excited also but he had to play it cool for the time being.

"Don't brag too much to your friends that you got my number." She smiled.

"Nah it ain't even like that."

"Uh huh!" Melissa said sarcastically.

Julani smiled and walked away. He walked over to his friends and they were happy as you could imagine.

"Man you pulled Melissa Moore? You a lucky ass nigga Lani." Jeff said. Jeff acted as if he had pulled the number. Julani just smiled.

"Yeah, she is fine as hell with a nice little petite frame. She kind of reminds me of that fine ass Internet girl Angel Lola Luv. With that gorgeous face but that small frame." Jeff replied.

"She's fine nigga but you kind of pushing it saying she as fine as Angel Lola Luv. But she is fine then a muthafucka." Chris commented.

He met Chris during his time at Cal State Long Beach. They had become good friends after having a few classes together.

"She's up there with her though!" Julani said.

"When are ya'll going out, that is what I want to know?" Jeff eagerly asked.

"Maybe this weekend, man she knew all kinds of shit about me. Did she come and ask you anything about me?"

"Not to me!" Jeff said.

"Me either!" Chris said.

"That's a little bit of a change for you Julani, she got bigger titties than she got ass. Don't get me wrong she does have a nice ass but you usually like them bigger." Jeff said.

"I know but that pretty ass face makes me consider the whole ass thing. Then again nah I still like a gang of ass. She got enough for me to work with though." Julani chuckled.

They laughed a little while longer then broke up the circle to go to class. Julani couldn't wait until the weekend for his date with Melissa.

He decided to take her to the Olive Garden for dinner. They were having a good time laughing and joking. He thought Melissa had a great sense of humor to be a 'beauty queen'. She could joke and act silly like his first love Deidre could. He took her home that night and walked her to her door. They hesitated then gently kissed each other on the lips. But Julani had to kiss her pretty ass again. So he came back and grabbed her by the waist and French kissed her good. She smiled as if she couldn't wait for him to do that. That

87

was the wonderful closure to their first date. It was everything he had hoped for.

The first time they had sex was exactly two weeks after the first date. He brought her back to his new apartment with no furniture. It was a nice two bedroom, two-bathroom spread with ceiling fan, dishwasher and garbage disposal. Julani was able to move some of his things into his bedroom from his mother's place. One of the main things he took was his bed.

Julani and Melissa had gotten into a hot passionate French kissing exchange. He started touching her all over her body. He got her down to her panties and bra. As he went to take off her panties he got a whiff of something he didn't like. It smelled like fish at the Redondo Beach Pier. He pulled her panties down anyway because lust was dominating his logic.

"Are you sure you are not on your period?" Julani asked trying to hide his disgust.

Julani considered that sometimes a woman might slip up and have an odor because of her period.

"No I have been off my period for about a week." She replied.

Well shit, she doesn't have an excuse Julani thought. Instead of killing the mood he opted for them to take a shower together.

"It's more romantic!"

She agreed and they quickly got into the shower. He washed her up and down like he used to do Deidre. He cleaned her vagina with soap and water wishing he had vinegar. But it did the job for the time. They dried off and he put on the condom and got busy. He had thought about going down on her but the previous odor made him consider otherwise. They made love on his bed and he tried to enjoy it as much as he could. They say sex is mostly mental and Julani wasn't as excited as he thought that he would be. Her not being up on her hygiene was a turn-off. Julani didn't totally hold it against her because he knew he could have caught her on a bad day. But it definitely messed up the mood for him that day. He made sure she had her orgasm then he went into the bathroom. He poured his semen in the toilet. He was so thrown off that he couldn't cum.

Instead of having blue balls he just released his sperm in the toilet. He quickly took her home so he could ponder on his problem. He decided to talk to Jeff about it when he got home.

"You mean to tell me Melissa Moore's pussy stank?" Jeff laughed aloud.

"It did today; I might have just caught her on a bad day." Julani explained.

"Nah nigga, I remember when I met this girl Tameka who stayed in Linwood. She was fine as hell. The first time I kissed her, her breath smelled like hot garbage. The cold thing was that when I was kissing her I could taste her badass breath. Lani she was so fine that it brought me to tears to find out she had halitosis." Jeff explained.

"What did you do?"

"Nigga I never called her ass again. When she would call I would tell my mom to say I wasn't home. I never told her why I just stopped fucking with her."

"I ain't going to break up with Melissa over that because it could have been just today." Julani replied. He felt he had to defend her honor.

"The first time ya'll having sex and she couldn't make sure her twat smelled right. Come on Lani, you're making excuses for her. If she knew that her pussy didn't smell right she would have not gave you the drawers. Women with good hygiene are conscious about that kind of shit. You remember Lisa's cousin Lanette...?"

"Yeah nigga, I remember Lanette; what her pussy stinks too?" Julani asked with a hint of sarcasm.

"Nah nigga, one time I was about to hit and her scrunchy that was holding her pony tail got damp. I smelled the dampness and didn't say anything. She noticed the smell just as quick as I did and took it out of her hair. She was like 'ugh this Scrunchy smell damp!' This was something as trivial as a thing that holds your ponytail in place and I never smelled a bad odor from Lanette. Some women just haven't been taught how to clean themselves properly. You gon' have to cut her loose, dog." Jeff somberly admitted.

"As fine as she is I can't do that. I'll give her another chance and if I get the same result I won't mess with her anymore." Julani persisted.

"Alright dog that is on you. But first impressions are the best impressions. But I will let you find out for yourself." Jeff surrendered.

For weeks Julani would take the homecoming queen out. He would eat lunch with her in the cafeteria so people could see they were an item. But he wouldn't bring her home for sex.

"Baby we haven't been to your house for no hanky-panky except for that one day. Don't you want to make love to me?" Melissa seductively asked.

"Yeah baby, I just don't want our relationship to be built around sex that's all. I was hoping we could learn each other and grow mentally also." He explained.

"Yeah but I'm not saying let us have sex everyday but maybe a couple times a week is healthy for a college couple." Melissa persisted.

"Yeah, okay well when we finish classes today we can go back to my house for a little while and we can make up for lost time."

"Baby now that is what I'm talking about. Give me some sugar." Melissa smiled.

He met Melissa in front of her class when it was over. She had on this overalls outfit with a pink shirt showing her cleavage. The shirt had 'Spoiled' written on it. She had on pink and white sneakers to match her shirt. Julani liked the way Melissa would dress it was sexy but stylish. It was cold outside so Julani couldn't wait to get in the car and turn on the heater. He had to make a few stops before they got back to his place. He came across a part of Long Beach where the sewers smelled bad. He had to endure the smell until he passed the area but he had grown use to it. As he passed the area he realized that he still smelled another stench. The further away from the area he got the more concerned he was about the smell. It didn't smell like a sewer anymore. It was a familiar smell that he couldn't put his finger on. He got to thinking maybe it was something he left in his car that had spoiled. He searched for the smell in vain then finally chose to ignore it.

"Can I change the CD in your CD Player?" Melissa asked.

"Yeah sure the CD case is on the floor on the passenger side." Julani pointed to the floor on the passenger side.

That was when he glanced down at the passenger side floor. She had taken off her sneakers. He discovered the smell that was familiar to him. It was the smell of funky feet. He couldn't believe it when he realized it was her feet that had that stench. He was too through. This was 'three much' he thought himself. She was so into the music she put the CD in the radio without a care in the world.

"I'm going to go ahead and take you home. I realized that I had something to do and I almost forgot." Julani lied.

"Oh okay, well hopefully I can see you tomorrow?" Melissa playfully pouted.

Not on your life Julani thought to himself. He didn't respond to her question he just kept driving. He was trying to concentrate on getting her home and enduring the smell of her feet. He made sure to crack the window instead of packing in all that heat and odor. Now he had all he needed to make sure that he wouldn't mess with this woman ever again. It was over in his mind but he didn't know how to tell her. He glanced a few times at her while she kept staring at him. She knew there was another reason for him not wanting to go back to his place. Her eyes focusing on him made him feel guilty but he chose to ignore his guilt. He thought that it would be spiteful to break up with her then tell her that her feet stink. He gave a smirk while thinking about it.

"What's so funny?"

"Nothing I was just thinking about something."

He dropped her off at home and never called her again.

12
DREAMS DO COME TRUE

Julani went weeks trying to avoid Melissa. Finally she trapped him in one of the university hallways. He realized that she had never been dumped. It was hard to believe that any of her ex-boyfriends hadn't told her about her hygiene problem. Since she was desperate to have closure he considered telling her. He considered how he could tell her without hurting her feelings. He stood in front of her in the hallway contemplating what he should say.

"So what do you got to say Julani, you have been avoiding me for all this time now you have nothing to say?" Melissa demanded.

"Uh, I don't know what to say Melissa. I just don't think that we make a good couple."

"Bullshit, you're going to have to come better than that. You know how many niggas would love to take your place?" She snapped.

"They can have you." Julani mumbled.

"What did you say?" She heard him but couldn't believe her ears.

"Look Melissa I need to go. You have a good life; I don't think we are meant for one another." Julani said. He walked away waving his hand as if to dismiss her.

She grabbed his arm firmly and wouldn't let go. Julani's anger was beginning to simmer. Some women can't stand rejection even worse than men, Julani thought. She turned him around so that she could look at him face to face. Julani kept his head down so he couldn't make eye contact.

"You are going to just pass me up Julani? What I don't look good enough for you anymore? Am I not a dime piece?" She arrogantly espoused.

"A dime piece whose pussy stinks." Julani blurted out.

That very moment he wished he could have taken it back. He finally looked her in her face and he could see the hurt. Now he felt bad.

"Fuck you nigga!" She yelled

The hallway echoed her pain. A Professor walked into the hallway to close the door. The Professor looked at the couple and put her finger to her mouth. Both of them were quiet for the moment. Julani didn't have much to say because he thought he had said too much already. Melissa on the other hand was still in shock off of what he said. Julani could tell that she wanted to cry. But she dared not give him the satisfaction. Julani didn't want the satisfaction. His anger and his eagerness to get away from her was what made him lose his discipline. They stood there for a couple of moments in silence. Finally Julani just walked away without saying a word.

He didn't hear from Melissa ever again. He was hoping that she was fine or hadn't gone crazy. Don't flatter yourself he told himself. This was emotionally stressful for him as well. No matter what he had done he could not find the right woman. Every woman that he dealt with had been a headache one way or another. Maybe he was getting karma for what he did to Lisa and Deidre. Maybe he hadn't lived down the damage he had done to those girls. Time will tell.

While Julani was watching television and feeling sorry for himself, Jeff walked in. He had just come in from a date with Sherise. He had been dating her on and off for years and now she was back from Howard University for good. For the last two months that was all Jeff talked about. Sherise this and Sherise that. She had come over a few times but only when Jeff wanted to run in and out. But it was something different about Jeff this time around. He had plenty of women through high school and college but Sherise was something special to him. First thing Julani was able to notice was that he never referred to her as one of his bitches. He always called her his little woman. Others things like when he walked in the door he would ask if she called. Any other time Jeff would just look on the caller ID or check the answering machine. Only time he didn't ask if she called was if he had just left being with her. It was definitely a change for Jeff.

"What's up Lani my nigga? What's happening with you?" Jeff approached in a jovial mood.

"Damn, you sound like you just won the lottery. What? You've just came back from being with Sherise?" Julani asked. He slid up from the couch.

"Nah, Julani this was a solo mission. I got to tell you something dog." Jeff said with anticipation.

"What's up?"

"I want to ask Sherise to marry me." Jeff blurted out. He pulled out a small suede black box.

He opened the box and showed it to Julani. Julani saw the ring and couldn't believe his eyes. It must have cost him a fortune.

"Man, that is a beautiful ring; you must have paid a lot of money for it?" Julani remarked.

"I paid two grand for it. I used the money that I was saving to get my rims." Jeff jittered.

Julani knew right then and there that Jeff must have really loved Sherise. He had been talking about those rims for a while. He cancelled dates and did side hustles so that he could get those rims. Now he spent it on an engagement ring. For the first time Julani seen his best friend in love.

"Congratulations dog that is a beautiful thing you're doing my man. I hope I can find someone that can make me feel the way Sherise makes you feel." Julani smiled.

"You will Julani, you will! I'm going to tell you man dreams really come true, they really come true. I have been going to church with Sherise and her family and I love it. Since she's already had her degree in Business Administration she is here to stay. And the church we go to, the preacher is really teaching something. He ain't just hooping and hollering. Her family is real cool. I'm not going to lie to you even Shayla is real cool."

"How is sexy ass Shayla, I haven't seen her in years?"

"She looks the same to me. She was engaged once but it didn't work out but she got a four-year-old son by the nigga. He seems like he's pretty cool based on what I seen."

"Well I hope I don't have to ask about being the best man?"

"Ah nigga that goes without saying. But she has to say yes first. I think she is but you never know."

They embraced each other as brothers and friends. That fast he had forgotten about all his woman problems. If a player like Jeff could find true love there must be someone out there for him. This must be a sign for better times.

The next day Jeff came barging into the house. He was yelling and jumping up and down as if he really had won the lottery.

"She said yes, she said yes!" Jeff shouted.

Julani jumped up and joined in the celebration. They were dancing around making noises as if they had won the Super Bowl. They kept doing it until the neighbors downstairs pounded on the ceiling for them to stop.

"Ay my nigga, I bought this bottle of Champaign so we could celebrate if she said yes." Julani said. He pulled out a bottle of champagne he had hidden in the freezer.

"Thank you Lani, you are the best friend anyone could have. Let's have a few drinks and relax for the rest of the night because I am engaged."

They drank the bottle until it was empty. They were lying around the apartment with a nice buzz reminiscing on past things. Bringing up past relationships and old flings.

"Ay Lani I meant to tell you I seen Deidre a few weeks back. I didn't know if you wanted to know because you were dating Melissa's stankin ass at the time. But she asked about you. Sherise and I were passing through Paramount and saw her at this grocery store. She was still fine then a muthafucka. Sherise was a little jealous until I told her she was your ex-girlfriend. She says she goes to Northridge and she was just in town for break."

"Now if I would have stuck with her we would probably be married or engaged. Now that was a soul mate I fucked over." Julani was slurring his words at this point.

"Yeah that's right you, fucked up with her when you started messing around with big booty Lisa. Whatever happened to her?" Jeff asked out of curiosity.

"She dances at some strip club now. Bruce seen her when he went and he couldn't wait to call me. He was saying some club off in Hawthorne. You want to go see her for your Bachelor party?"

"Why would I want to go see a bitch *you fucked?*"

They both started laughing out loud. The champagne had gotten to them and they both knew it.

"Then what is it you want to do for your bachelor party?"

"Surprise me!"

"Ah nigga you tripping but I will think of something."

"You know Sherise had me thinking today about using the word nigga. She was saying that when she was at Howard, Blackness was a beautiful thing. She said that Black people had a sense of pride when you go to the Black colleges. I'm going to try to stop using the word nigga in my vocabulary."

Julani was touched by the comment. He knew without a doubt that Jeff had fallen in love. This was a woman that he was willing to change for. If a woman can inspire a man to be better she got him. She didn't force him to surrender he did it voluntarily. A lot of women miss the boat when they think they can force a man to be better. He has to be willing to do it for himself. She just was being her sweet and kind self and she made Jeff strive for something he hadn't strived for. At that point Julani knew that Sherise was sacred to Jeff. In that example he wanted to follow his heart.

Julani fell asleep on the couch dreaming of what he wanted in a woman. What he expected his queen to be like. Jeff lied next to him on the floor dreaming about the woman he was about to marry. Julani and Jeff were both in a drunken heavenly state. If life could be this wonderful all the time there wouldn't be any sorrow in the world. Before you knew it they were both snoring loudly on the living room floor.

The following morning they woke up to the phone ringing. They both were disoriented from the liquor. Finally Jeff was able to reach the cordless first. It was right next to him lying on the floor.

"Hello?"

"Congratulations, my nigga, Terri told me that you and Sherise are getting married. That is some tight ass shit my nigga." Bruce yelled through the phone.

Julani looked at Jeff asking who was calling at six in the fucking morning on a Saturday. He silently told Julani it was Bruce. Julani waved his hand and lied back down on the couch.

"So you married the girl of your dreams, huh nigga?" Bruce continued.

He was so loud that Julani could hear him through the phone.

"Yeah man, Sherise is the woman I have always wanted. I feel real good right now. Ay, but let me call you back a little later because it's six in the morning and I'm still sleepy. I'll hit you back when I wake up."

"Alright dog, but congratulations again. That is some tight shit. But you got me into some shit because now Terri is talking that marriage shit. Just holler at me later and I will tell you all about it."

"Alright later!"

Jeff cut the ringer off and went back into his slumber. Julani had already went back to sleep.

13
HOMIE LOVER FRIEND

The day had finally come for Jeff and Sherise to say their vows. A year and a half passed. Julani and Jeff both graduated from California State University of Long Beach. Julani was already working for Fox Television. Jeff landed a job in the accounting department at a Johnson & Johnson company. They were doing well to be fresh out of college. Sherise graduated from Howard in three years so she already was a schoolteacher at Wilson High School on the Far East side of Long Beach. The school district allowed her to work without getting credentials but now she had them. It was a beautiful time for everyone and now the wedding day finally arrived.

Julani spent his entire Saturday getting groomed and preparing for the Sunday wedding. Jeff bought an all white with silver trimming tuxedo that buttoned up to his neck. Julani decided to rent his tuxedo but his was also white with silver trimming. The wedding was done at a park out in San Pedro. Sherise's sister Shayla would be the maid of honor. The seating arrangement was packed on both sides. Jeff invited his grandparents, cousins, aunts and uncles and all his friends from junior high school, high school and college. It appeared as though Sherise had done the same. Sherise even invited people from Howard University that Julani met that Saturday afternoon at the last wedding rehearsal. One of her friends was a good-looking Jamaican girl that graduated with her. Sherise introduced her as Malika. Malika was looking at Julani with all smiles.

"So you are the best man that I have heard so much about." Malika said with a thick Jamaican accent.

"It is nice to meet you!" Julani smiled.

Julani seen how her eyes scanned his body up and down and he was flattered. Sherise told him Malika would be in town until Tuesday. Julani was hoping to hook up with her before her flight back to D.C. As for now he would have to calm his lust because the wedding was priority. He made sure he was able to contact Malika at her hotel and left it alone until the wedding was over.

Slowly the bridesmaids walked down the pathway to the music of Jodeci's 'Forever My Lady'. It was a song that Jeff and Sherise played when they first made love to each other as teenagers. Shayla and Julani then walked down the aisle. Julani couldn't help but to admire how good she looked in her dress. She smiled at him also admiring how he looked in his tuxedo. The Groom walked out and he was as cool as he wanted to be. Considering that he was making a life altering decision Jeff seemed relaxed. It was borderline arrogance. He finally reached the alter and shook hands with Julani. The bride came out shortly with her father escorting her down the aisle. Julani didn't want to be disrespectful but he thought Sherise really looked beautiful. He never really paid attention to her because he always seen her as his homeboy's woman. But this day Julani saw the beauty in her that Jeff had been seeing for years. He was proud of Jeff. He smiled while she made her way up to the Alter.

Sherise and Jeff both wrote out their vows. Julani started daydreaming as they said the wedding vows. He looked at that segment of the wedding to be for the bride and groom. Finally they asked the Best Man to hand over the ring.

"I now pronounce you man and wife. You may kiss the bride!"

Everyone started clapping as they walked down the aisle. Julani began to relax once Jeff and Sherise made it out the door. He wanted to go home and change for the wedding reception. He hurried home to change into his two-piece outfit. He made it back to the reception in an hour. The bride and the groom hadn't made it to the reception yet. He figured they would take a little longer. It surprised him when they arrived only thirty minutes after he did. When they walked in the door Shayla was close behind her sister.

When they made it to the table designated for people in the wedding Shayla walked up to Julani.

"Julani, you don't know how good you look in that two piece. You make me want to bite you."

"You are knocking people out with that evening gown you're wearing. I didn't think that someone could make silver look so good. How have you been?"

"I've been doing fine. I can't complain since I've opened my own Salon."

"I heard you just opened your Salon in North Long Beach. That is beautiful Shay, I'm really happy for you." He smiled.

"You are one to talk, I heard you work for Fox Television now. You are in the big time now. And you are still sexy as hell. I know you got the women lined up for you to be their man."

"Shit I ain't the only one that is sexy as hell. You look just the same as you did seven years ago. Are you beating men off with a broom?"

"Well I hope that you can come back around and visit like you did a long time ago." She flirted

"How can I get in touch with you?" For Julani at that moment the air got thinner.

"Here is my business card and I will put my home and cell number on the back."

"Okay!"

"Matter of fact what are you getting into tonight? My daughter is with her father and I wanted to get something to drink a little later on." Shayla asked.

"Can't you get something to drink here at the reception?"

"Not just Champagne Julani, something stronger." She playfully frowned.

"Now I know you haven't turned into an alcoholic over the years?" Julani joked.

"Nah, but my daughter is with her father until the end of the week. I was hoping to get loose while she was gone." She winked at him.

"He must have pulled up right after the wedding to pick your daughter up?"

"Shiiit, I called that nigga right before I was walking down the aisle. He pulled up five minutes after we walked out the church. I knew he was going to take his sweet time so I told him that it was over before it was. His timing was perfect."

Julani laughed and started sipping on Champagne. He noticed that Malika kept staring at him while he sat at the table talking to Shayla. He wanted to be greedy tonight. He knew that Shayla was going to be ready for sex so he stuck with her. Some people never change. As for Malika he didn't know what to expect but he didn't want to count her totally out. The way he planned it was to appear as though he had to stay at the table next to Shayla. It was his subtle way of showing proper etiquette. But he made sure to give Malika eye contact so that she knew he was interested in her also. He figured that he could probably take her out on the town either Monday or Tuesday. As for tonight he was going to have a sex date with Shayla.

As he contemplated his maneuvers someone hitting the Champagne glasses interrupted his thoughts.

"It is now time for the Best Man and Maid of Honor to give their speeches." Sherise's aunt announced.

Julani indicated to Shayla that she should go first. She walked up to the podium looking lovely. Her face glowing with pride she began to speak into the microphone.

"I love my sister. This is the only sister I got and I am lucky to have her as my sister. In many ways we are different but our loyalty to one another is the same. Throughout the years not only has she been my sister but my friend. As a friend and the Maid of Honor I know that she has been waiting for this day for a long time. I am so happy for you girl..." Tears fell from Shayla's eyes.

"I hope you and Jeff have a beautiful life together. I love the both of you and God Bless this union."

Shayla walked over to Sherise to hug and kiss her. Tears were in both of their eyes as they embraced. How am I going to top that, Julani thought? He considered he shouldn't be thinking like that. Let me come from the heart and let the words flow appropriately he silently prayed. Shayla sat down next to him and he rose slowly to walk towards the podium.

"There are times in your life that will mark significant changes. You will feel the change suddenly and have to react accordingly. This is one of those changes I must admit for me. Because now not only do I have one best friend, I now have two best friends. Two of the most beautiful people I know have joined together forever. The day Jeff told me that he was going to propose to Sherise I saw love in his eyes. You see ladies and gentlemen I have known this man most of our lives. And I can truly say that he loves this woman with all his heart and soul. As his friend I will protect this union from anyone trying to harm it because I know that is what my friend would want me to do and because that is what I would be honored to do. I also love both of you and I also love that you have fallen in love with one another. Thank you for being my friend."

The crowd went into an uproar as he walked away from the podium. Julani's mother had tears coming down her face after his speech. He glanced over at Malika and she smiled at him with so much admiration. When he made it back to the table Shayla hugged and kissed him on the cheek. Once he was in his seat him and Jeff made eye contact and they shared a moment of mutual love and friendship. Sherise constantly thanked him as she kissed her hand and waived it at him.

Julani sat at the table after they cut the cake. He patiently waited for the guests to leave. When he saw Malika get up to leave he excused himself from the table. He acted as if he needed to go to the restroom. He made sure she was out the reception hall before he approached.

"Hey Malika are you headed back to your hotel room?"

"Yeah Julani, I'm tired but maybe you can stop by tomorrow."

"That will be excellent for me. What will be a good time to stop by?

102

"I would prefer in the afternoon because in the morning I wanted to sleep in and finish some paperwork."

"What do you do anyway Malika?"

"I am a lawyer for a small law firm in Washington D.C. I just started but they allowed me to visit Los Angeles for Sherise's wedding. I was hoping that you might show me around out here before I head back?" She smiled.

"That would be my pleasure." Julani replied.

She smiled and wrote down her hotel room on the back of her business card. I got two business cards today Julani thought. She hugged him and kissed him on the cheek.

"I'll see you tomorrow I hope?" She began walking away.

"Boy, you can charm the pants off of Jamaican women *too*?" Julani was startled by his mother's words. She smiled at him when he turned around.

"Give me a hug boy, so I can go home and get some sleep. I love you and you be careful with Sherise's sister she has been on you all night." His mother gave a sly grin.

Julani hugged his moms and chuckled. Nothing gets past her. He used the restroom and walked back into the reception hall. He saw Shayla talking to one of her aunts. He walked over to Shayla and spoke to both of them.

"Are you ready to go?" Shayla asked.

"Sure, whenever you are."

Shayla grabbed her heels from under the table. She hugged her aunt then walked out the door with Julani. She couldn't wait to get out of the reception hall. By that time it was ten-thirty in the evening.

"So what bar were you talking about going to tonight?" Julani asked.

"I'm tired; how about I follow you back to your house and we kick it?"

"Okay that's cool, follow me."

They drove back to where Julani and Jeff once lived together. Jeff had already moved out and had prepared to buy a house with Sherise. Julani kept the apartment and took over the rent.

He bought new furniture and a sound system for the living room. His bedroom set was new but he had it for about nine months. Then he decked the kitchen out with some help from his mother. His two-bedroom apartment looked nice and he was proud to have company. Julani pulled up into his designated parking space and indicated to Shayla to find a parking space. He parked so that he could escort her from her car. When she found a parking space he waited for her to parallel-park then he opened her door.

"You always were a gentleman."

"Thank you, Thank you. Who was that you were talking to at the reception your mother's sister?" Julani asked.

"No that was my daddy's sister Aunt Linda. She arranged everything for the wedding. You know one of those overzealous religious types. Nothing is done right unless she does it. Shit I was glad when you walked up because she would have started getting into church and all kinds of shit."

Julani laughed as they walk up to his doorstep. He lets her in then walked in quickly to turn on the lights.

"Get comfortable while I straighten up."

His house was already clean he just wanted to burn some of his incense. Julani grabbed his lighter from out of the junk drawer. Most black families have a junk drawer usually in the kitchen and he was no different. He started lighting everything that could make the apartment smell better. While he was in the bedroom he heard Shayla cut on the television. He got a little more comfortable in his basketball shorts and matching top. He slid on his new house slippers and walked back into the living room. By that time Shayla was raiding his refrigerator. He laughed while the news was showing something humorous.

"What's so funny?" She yelled from the kitchen.

"Something on T.V."

She walked back into the living room butt naked. Her body hadn't loss any of its appeal since seven years ago. She had a daughter since then and her titties didn't sag. In fact they looked bigger than he remembered.

"What was on T.V.?" She asked again. Acting as if she wasn't standing butt naked in front of him.

Julani instantly grew a bulge in his pants. He touched her on her stomach and she moaned. He then started kissing her passionately. He grabbed her big ass firmly. It was just as firm as he remembered. He slid his shorts off while still kissing her. He then picked her up and took her into the room and laid her on the bed. He pulled a condom from out of the drawer and slid it on fast. He smelled her vagina and became more aroused by the sweet smell of her aroma. Now this is how a woman is supposed to smell. He began sucking on her clitoris with hard long strokes. She grabbed the back of his head as she kept grinding on his mouth. She was going so fast that it appeared that she had cum already. At this point he figured she probably had a small orgasm.

He lifted his head up and climbed on top of her hot perspired body. He didn't waste any time and quickly slid inside of her. They start fucking to the music Julani had playing on the radio by his bed. The radio station was playing 'Do Me Baby' by Prince. They kissed and fucked and kissed and fucked. She turned him over and she got on top. She began riding him with her head turning in different directions. She started screaming 'oh yeah' as she let her hair down. Julani grabbed her ass cheeks firmly and pushed inside of her. They were letting the music guide their movements. And as if timing couldn't be more perfect they came at the same time. It was number two for Shayla. Julani lied next to her after she collapsed, breathing hard. She started wiping sweat from his face like he was her child.

"That has always been a beautiful thing you and I shared." Julani commented.

"I know, even when you were younger and I would teach you things you were a fast learner. Now you are new and improved." She teased.

"After all these years we linked up again."

"Yeah, we will probably always have that bond. We shared some good times together. We will probably always be each other's Homie, Lover, Friend. Now that my sister and your best friend are married we might see more of each other."

"I hope so!" Julani replied.

He rolled over to kiss on her naked body. Julani had to admit he was weak for this woman. Maybe because she was the first he ever had? Or they had a bond that they always had and never knew it. They kept making love for the rest of the night. They didn't stop until daybreak. They were making up for lost time.

14
GO SEE THE DOCTOR

The following morning Julani fixed a nice breakfast. Shayla woke up a little later than he did. She walked into the living room to the smell of waffles and eggs. She was still butt naked when she came out of the bathroom. But it didn't surprise Julani because Shayla was always an exhibitionist. Even though he liked that about her that wasn't what he liked about her most. What he liked about Shayla the most was how sweet she could be. She never really had a bad attitude. Shayla could break up with you in a nice way. No matter the circumstances she was a lady about everything. It was refreshing because Julani dealt with a lot of black women that mistook being strong with being mean. He realized that he never stopped loving her. It was a maternal hold she had on him because of her teaching him intimacy. He knew that he wasn't *in love* with her. But he loved her. He was happy to be in her presence once again.

"So what is on your agenda today, Shayla?" Julani asked.

"Nothing really, I will probably go home and get some rest after I clean up my shop. I had to do my sister's hair for her wedding then do mine. What are you planning to get into today?"

"I really don't know yet, I am undecided."

"Uh huh, you probably plan to hook up with Sherise's Jamaican friend. She was looking at you all night. And you pretended like you were going to the restroom last night." She slyly smiled.

"I did go to the restroom last night."

"Julani we are friends so you don't have to lie to me."

"I know Shayla, we might hang out a little later but that depends."

"On what?"

107

"On how late she wants to hook up. Other than that I plan on relaxing for the day."

"You should take her to the Santa Monica Promenade or Sunset Boulevard out in Hollywood."

"I don't even know if we are going anywhere."

"Well those are some suggestions if you change your mind." Shayla mockingly replied.

They both started laughing. Julani had the breakfast laid out thick and they both talked until they finished eating. Shayla went home shortly afterwards. She could easily take a shower at his house but she didn't have a change of clothes. They kissed each other goodbye and promised to see one another soon. Julani took his time getting in the shower. He liked Shayla's smell on him. Her perfume was still in the air long after she left. And he smelled her all over his body. It was a pleasant smell that he chose to bask in for a time. He didn't take a shower until noon. He groomed himself hoping everything went as planned with the Jamaican girl. He called her around one in the afternoon. She eagerly picked up her phone hoping it was him. Julani could picture her smiling through the phone.

"Well lovely lady I was hoping we could have that night on the town you promised me."

"You mean the one you promised me." She laughed.

"Well I am a man of my word. Is this the Renaissance hotel by L.A.X.?"

"Yes it is, are you familiar with this area?"

"Yes I am, I can be in front of your hotel in about thirty to forty-five minutes. However you like I can go to your room or I can meet you downstairs in the lobby."

"I can be outside by the time to you've made it here."

"Okay, I'm on my way?"

Julani quickly threw together his two-piece outfit and Stacy Adams. He put on some of his best cologne and rushed out the door. It was amazing even to Julani how he had sex that morning but was excited about the prospect of getting some again that night. But it was something exotic about Malika that turned him on. She was small up top but she made up for it in legs, thighs, hips and ass. She was a very conservative dresser, which was always a turn on to Julani. She was actually the lightest Jamaican woman he had ever seen.

Julani pulled up to her hotel parking lot in thirty-five minutes flat. She smiled when he pulled up showing all thirty-two teeth. She had a beautiful smile with pearly white evenly spaced teeth. She didn't give him time to get out the car and be a gentleman. She climbed into the passenger seat of Julani's car still smiling. Her brown one piece dress was casual but sexy. He quickly complimented her and they started driving towards the beach. She started the conversation immediately.

"So how is it in the television business? Do you meet a lot of stars?"

"Not in my department, I specialize in dealing with marketing and putting in commercial time slots." He replied.

"That sounds interesting; do you like what you do?"

"Very much, I feel truly blessed to land this job at my age. Besides, my mother brags all the time about her only son being in the television business."

"You are an only child?" She asked. It was a tone of surprise in her voice.

"Yeah, why did you say it like that?"

"Only child people are usually spoiled. But you don't take me as that type."

"Well in some ways I am and in other ways I am not. I don't mistreat people who are less fortunate than me but I may indulge in things too much."

"Such as?"

"I don't know maybe clothes, my car and jewelry."

"Just like the typical Black man?"

"What does that suppose to mean?"

"The things that are least important are what we have a tendency to invest in." She replied.

"Well I agree in most cases but I believe I have my priorities straight. Since I am an only child my mother never minds helping me with trivial things. But she is also the first to tell me to create an egg nest for the future."

"Well that is good to know. So where are you taking me?" She asked while surveying the area.

"I'm taking you down to the Santa Monica Promenade. They have rides and arcades. We can walk and talk while we are down there. They also have shops down on the street. I am hoping you enjoy it. Can I ask you a personal question?"

"Sure!"

"Are there a lot of Jamaicans with light complexion because you are the first I have ever seen?"

"That is because you have never been to Jamaica. You have heard of Bob Marley right well he was light skin." She replied with attitude.

"Yeah that's true I guess I have never seen one in person. I was just asking out of curiosity that's all, I hope I didn't offend you."

"No not at all! To tell you the truth I am actually from a small island called Barbados. It easy for me to just say I am Jamaican because that is what most people are familiar with."

"Did you ever become Rastafarian? I knew a guy in college that was Rastafarian. He said that they believe that Halle Selassie is the Messiah. He said that for years Jamaica had a drought and it started raining the day Halle Selassie arrived in Jamaica. Have you heard anything about that?" Julani pried.

"Yeah I have heard of that but I am not Rastafarian. I knew some that smoked reefer all the time. But that wasn't my crowd."

They pulled up to the parking lot. Julani paid for parking then found a place to park. When she got out the car he really liked what he saw. She wore a brown loose but form fitting one-piece dress. With her walking side by side with him he thought they made a good couple. Her height was just right. If she wore heels she wouldn't be taller than him. They both were conservative dressers. And they both carried themselves with pride and dignity. This was a woman that was on the ball Julani thought.

They first walked the promenade, looking into shops. Malika bought a few souvenirs. They finally decided to walk down to the beach pier after a couple of hours. The next hour they played video games and got weird art drawn. They laughed and talked while they ate pizza. Then finally they got on the Ferris wheel.

"I wonder if we should have eaten that pizza after we got on the Ferris wheel." Malika asked.

"I know, my stomach felt a little crazy too but now that we are off I don't feel it anymore. Do you need to sit down?"

"No it was while we were on the Ferris wheel also. I just thought that it might have been a smoother ride if we would have eaten after the ride." She frowned.

"I don't know, are you ready to head back to the car it is getting dark."

"Yeah, it is about that time we start heading back. But I must say Julani I had a wonderful time."

"I did too. I wish that we could spend more time together."

"Well we will definitely keep in touch and maybe we can get another chance to spend together. We can exchange numbers before I head back to D.C."

"That will be fine."

They continued to enjoy one another's company while they walked to the car. Now she was giving him the look. The look that implied she was sexually attracted to him. The same one she gave him the night before at the wedding reception. Once they were in the car Julani decided to set the mood. He threw in his Tony Tone Toni CD. The CD with 'It never rains in Southern California.' She felt the vibe and responded by touching his hand. He glanced over at her and she smiled. He was totally hooked on her smile. It literally made his knees weak. But he played it cool. They made it back to her hotel in twenty-five minutes flat.

"Would you like to come upstairs for a little while?" She seductively asked.

"Sure, why not."

Once he parked they walked upstairs holding hands. They were acting silly with one another but not really talking. They took the elevator to the seventh floor. When Julani walked into the room he was impressed.

111

"This is a nice hotel room."

"It should be for $185 a night. Have a seat anywhere you like."

Julani sat down on her couch that was close to her bed. He didn't want to assume he was able to sit on her bed regardless of what she said. He wanted to have proper etiquette with Malika. She changed into something a little more comfortable. She put on a long blue silk nightgown that still showed her curves. Julani had to briefly gasp for air. She looked extremely good and his hormones were going crazy.

"Would you like some wine?"

"Yeah sure." Julani nervously responded.

She brought in the wine and sat next to him on the couch. She sat close to him so that the sexual tension could be created.

"Are you okay Julani? Maybe I can do something to make you feel more comfortable."

Without hesitation she got on her knees and unzipped his pants. He sat there quietly as she undressed him. She pulled his already stiffened penis from out of his trousers and put her lips around the tip of his manhood. This was different for Julani because she gave head like a professional. She treated his dick like she was in love with kissing it. He laid his head back and let her take over. She kept going and going like the energizer bunny. Then right when he was about to cum she grabbed his arm. She lifted up her nightgown and lied on the bed. He quickly pulled a condom from out of his wallet then slipped it on. As he penetrated she wrapped her legs around his body. He started kissing on her neck and breast. She had given him head for too long so he was going to have to pass on tongue kissing her.

He was about to cum faster than he wanted to, so he changed positions. He let her get on top and she started going wild. She was in surprisingly good shape. After awhile Julani thought Malika had too much energy. She wouldn't stop. Then with one sudden shriek she laid on his chest. She had finally cum. He hadn't gotten a chance to cum so he turned her over on her stomach. When he stuck it in she felt a little dry so it was kind of difficult to put it in her

112

vagina. When he finally penetrated he quickly felt himself about cum. He pulled out and realized that the condom had broken. He spilled semen all on her ass and legs. She gave a small sexual moan as if she enjoyed it. He got up from the bed feeling dizzy and exhausted.

"I thought you put on a condom?"

"I did put on a condom but it broke inside of you." Julani explained.

"Are you okay, you look dizzy?"

"Well that was some work out that's all. Can I go to your bathroom?"

She pointed to the bathroom. He went into the bathroom then grabbed a washcloth and soap to wash up. He would take a shower when he got home. When he came out of the bathroom he quickly got dressed. He was ready to go after that episode. She didn't mind because she was through with him anyway.

"Well let me go and I will call you when you get to D.C."

"Okay Julani, you take care." She smiled.

Julani rushed out the door without knowing why. He thought about her for a couple of days. For some reason her smell was still on him even though he had taken a shower. It was a pleasant smell he just didn't understand why it lingered. It was now Wednesday and he still thought about her.

"Hey Julani where are you going to lunch today?" His white co-worker Matt asked. His thoughts were interrupted at this point.

"I was thinking Yoshinoya, how about that?"

"That's cool dude, I'll drive today!" Matt replied.

Julani liked Matt because he was one of those white boys that liked Hip Hop. Twelve-thirty came and they were headed out the door.

"Ay Matt, let me use the restroom before we go?"

Julani ran into the restroom because he had to pee badly. He ran to the stall and stood there for a second without his urine coming out. He pushed harder then finally something came out. When it came out he started screaming. His knees felt weak and he started pissing on the floor. He was hurting terribly and couldn't do

113

anything about it. Why am I hurting so bad Julani thought? Then his second thought was Malika.

15
WOMEN VS. BITCHES

"Hello?"

"Hello, can I speak to Malika?"

"This is Malika, who is this?"

"This is Julani, do you remember me?

"How can I forget you since last weekend? I just wasn't expecting you to call so soon. What's going on?"

"Well actually I am calling you with some bad news."

"Something happened with Sherise and Jeff?"

"No nothing like that. I was calling to tell you to go see a doctor. You gave me gonorrhea."

"That's bullshit; maybe one of your California bitches gave you gonorrhea. Don't call me with that kind of shit Julani." She sneered. For the first time he could hear a hint of her Jamaican accent.

"I am not lying to you. You are the only girl that I had sex with and the condom broke. I couldn't have gotten it from anyone but you" Julani explained.

There was a moment of silence on the phone.

"I know this can be embarrassing but you should get checked out." He continued. "Look Malika I am not trying to hurt you but I am sure about what I'm talking about."

"Okay, I will go check it out. Goodbye!"

"Goodbye!"

"Julani wait!"

"Yeah what's up?"

"You handled that like a real man should. I apologize for being so hostile but I appreciate the way you gave it to me."

"Well I know you didn't try to do this to me it just happened that way. Take care of yourself and I will make sure this is between you and me. Sherise and Jeff don't have to know anything about this." Julani replied.

"Thank you!" He heard a sigh of relief through the phone.

Since he had already taken his shot he felt better than before. Julani had finally gotten tired. This playing the field trying to experiment with different women in sex was hard work. The stress and the drama wasn't worth it. But some habits die hard. Julani had to face the fact that he was addicted to sex. He was officially a womanizer. Sex was his mission when he dealt with the opposite sex. He never had a woman with the exception of Deidre that he did everything with. But he knew he couldn't go back to her. Besides he was more mature and there would be different qualities he would look for nowadays. He contemplated this until he decided to go visit his mother. He hadn't seen her all this week and he needed to talk.

He drove over to his mother's house and let his self in. His mother was in the living room watching television.

"Hey Mama, I thought you were into that V.C. Andrews book. I didn't expect you to be watching T.V."

"Boy I finished 'Flowers in the Attic' last night. I plan on reading 'Pedals in the Wind' next week. What are you doing over here? And you didn't even call. What if Lawrence was over here?"

"I came to see you mama, how have you been?"

"I've been fine, what's wrong with you. Are you lonely now that you don't have your road dog anymore?"

"Where do you be learning this slang from?" Julani said surprised by his mom's wordplay.

"I hear it all the time; I tell you a lot of stuff is recycled. But don't avoid the question."

"I can't just want to see my mama? It gotta be a reason I come and visit except that I just want to see you?"

"Yeah, but popping up without calling is not like you. So I figured something was on your mind."

"Well I did want to talk to you. You know that Jamaican girl I met at the wedding?"

"Yeah, I remember her. Very attractive light skin woman, the one you were talking to in the hallway. I heard at the wedding that she was a lawyer."

"Yeah, well we messed around and I caught a disease from her."

"Boy you act like you don't have any common sense. You haven't heard of such a thing called condoms."

"I used a condom but it must have been defective because it broke."

"Well that is what you get for messing with a girl you barely met anyhow. Are you alright now?"

"Yeah, I'm fine now but Wednesday and Thursday was some ruff days for me. You wouldn't even think it would happen with a girl like that. She looked good, she smelled good and she carried herself with class. It blew me away to find out that she gave me that."

"When you don't really know these women they can make you believe anything they want you to believe. We as women practice deception better than any man could ever do. We will make a man believe that he is God on earth and he is the only one worthy of our love. But at the same time accept presents and gifts from many different men. Men want sex and women know it so they play all sorts of games to get what they want from men."

"But how do you know if you are dealing with a woman that is good for you? These women today are slicker than they were in your day."

"Time! You have to find out through time. Every person puts on the game face when they first start dating you. You don't show every woman your faults when she first meets you. But time will reveal all things. People can't hide who they really are forever. You young people are so used to getting everything fast like a microwave oven. Something achieved so easily is not really that valuable. You gave her all these compliments but she didn't think that much of herself to have sex with you and hadn't known you a week. You didn't think that much of yourself to have sex with a girl

117

you barely knew. But time and time that's what happens and you wonder why the right girl hasn't come yet."

"But mama I am a grown sexually active heterosexual man and I need some intimacy every now and then if you know what I mean." Julani protested.

"You need? You ain't any better than a drug addict that can't stay off of heroin. Love is what every person is entitled to."

"Well mama why haven't you married Lawrence, you love him don't you?" Julani challenged her.

"Very much and he has proposed but there are certain freedoms that I am not willing to give up right now. He owns his house and I own my condo and making those adjustments are too complicated for both of us right now. But we enjoy each other's company and are the best of friends."

"It is hard to get the pick of the litter nowadays. I don't know what to do about these women today." Julani continued to complain.

"Well the first thing you can do is change what is in you that makes you attract the type of women that you do. If you play in the gutter then you are going to get dirty, you know what I mean."

"I know, I know!" Julani somberly admitted.

"You have allowed yourself to become a monogamous slut. A real woman wouldn't tolerate that from you. These rappers call women bitches and whores but that is because the women they encounter think sex is their best asset. If they have a cute shape and sex appeal, they've been made to believe that they are worth their weight in gold. How can a woman like that satisfy your soul? How can she give you a family to be proud of when her attraction is mostly physical? Even men get tired of meaningless sex with a woman that doesn't bring anything else to the table. Right when he finds a woman that has more to offer than just that, he will be gone with the wind. Remember you told me that was your problem with that girl Lisa. You can do better than what you have been getting Julani baby. Be careful about your body, mind and soul."

He left his mother's house feeling better. His mother was right he could do better than what he was doing. His lack of self-esteem had allowed him to settle for sex instead of love. If he wanted to stop being with bitches he had to stop being a nigga. His life had to change for the better or he was going to go crazy.

The next day Jeff and Sherise had gotten back from their honeymoon. They were gone for a week and a half. Jeff gave Julani a call. After work Julani stopped by to hang out with his newlywed friend. He pulled up in front of Jeff's new house and Jeff was already outside. He had a glass in his hand when Julani walked up.

"So how was the honeymoon, I know you had a good time?" Julani asked. They shook hands and embraced.

"I had a real good time. Shit I wish I could have a stayed another week. Did you hook up with Shayla or Malika?"

"Both, Shayla and I had a good time together reminiscing and catching up. She has always been cool."

"I remember a time when you couldn't stand Shayla. That is good that you two are able to mend your differences." Jeff smiled.

"Yeah, I was young, dumb and full of cum back then. She needed a man more mature and so I got hurt when she broke up with me. As I got older I understood why she did what she did. Now we get along fine...

Ay, tell your wife I said hello. I am not trying to be rude standing outside and not going in to speak."

"Come on lets go inside so you can say hello."

They walked inside Jeff's new house and Sherise had already gone to work with decorations. Julani smiled as he scanned the room looking at the artwork. They painted the walls and put carpet on some of the floor. It was turning out to be real nice Julani thought.

"Man, you and Sherise are really putting this house together." He commented.

"Yeah, she concentrates on the decorations while I concentrate on painting and repairs. So far so good."

"How are you doing Julani it is so nice to see you." Sherise walked into the living room.

"How are you doing Sherise you surprised me." Julani laughed.

They hugged and everyone went into the living room. Jeff and Sherise talked about their trip and the wonderful honeymoon they had. They were upbeat and in good spirits. Julani felt the love in the room and yearned for the same thing. As they finish the story Julani's cell phone rings. He saw on the caller ID that it was Shayla. Julani excused himself from the room.

"Hello!"

"What are you doing tonight?"

"I have nothing planned why?"

"My daughter is with her father and I was hoping to spend a little time with you. Why are you whispering?" Shayla curiously asked.

"I'm at your sister's house and I didn't know if you wanted her to know you were calling me." Julani explained.

"Oh I don't care. Matter of fact let me speak to her for a moment."

Julani walked back into the living room and handed Sherise the cell phone. Sherise had a puzzled look on her face until Julani told her it's her sister. She grabbed the phone and started laughing right away. Jeff asked if that was Shay silently and Julani confirmed with a nod. While Sherise was in the other room they watched the basketball game.

"What, you plan on hooking up with Shayla tonight?" Jeff asked out of nowhere.

"Yeah probably, she said that her daughter is with her father. You think the Lakers are going to do something this year?" Julani asked.

"I hope so; it is about time we won another ring. Forget just making it to the playoffs." Jeff replied.

Sherise walked in with the cell phone. She handed it to Julani and sat down next to Jeff. Julani put the phone to his ear.

"Hello?" he said.

"I can meet you at your house in an hour. Is that cool?" Shayla asked.

"Yeah that's cool!"

Julani hung up the phone and got back into watching the game. It would only take him fifteen to twenty minutes to get home so he had time to kill. He chitchatted with Jeff and Sherise until Sherise went into the kitchen. She was going to ask him to stay for dinner but she knew her sister. Julani could smell the Beef Stroganoff cooking. He tried to ignore it. Finally after about thirty minutes he excused himself.

"Call me this weekend Lani, maybe we can get into something like bowling or shoot some pool." Jeff said.

"Yeah that will be cool. Holler at me Saturday night."

"Yeah, that will be good because Sherise has her book club that night at seven."

Julani rushed out the door-yelling goodbye to Sherise. He wanted to make sure everything was right for Shayla. His house was clean but he wanted to make sure everything smelled right. But when he pulled up to his house Shayla was pulling up also. They got out of the car at the same time.

"I thought you said an hour?" Julani asked while walking up to her.

"I am only about ten minutes early." Shayla playfully rolled her eyes.

"I couldn't just up and leave because it would have looked obvious being I just got off the phone with you."

"Trust me it was already obvious because my sister knows me. And if not Jeff would have told her anyway."

They both laughed. Julani grabbed her bag and escorted her upstairs. He got her inside and took her bags into the room. Shayla quickly undressed like she always did. But this time Julani wanted to talk first.

"Why didn't you and your husband work out if you don't mind me asking?"

After she raided his refrigerator she walked over to the table where he was sitting. She was totally nude but was relaxed as if she was in a nude colony.

"Well some men are too controlling for a woman like me. He wanted to monitor everything I did. He wanted to make sure the house was clean meticulously. He just thought that since I was his wife I should do everything that he wanted me to do. I know how to obey my husband but I seen my mother and father interact and my father let my mother be herself. He tried to take that away from me. We argued all the time. We get along better now that we are divorced. What made you ask me that?"

"Because you are so sweet I don't see a man wanting to leave you. If you were my wife I would fight hard to keep us together."

"Well Julani, you will find your true love and when you do I won't have the pleasure of spending my time with you. There are bitches and there are women and don't settle for a bitch because you have not yet found a woman."

"How can you tell the difference?"

"Women work with a man that is willing to work with her. Bitches look at men as the enemy. With that kind of perception how can they make a good teammate? Now some men are the enemy but men are too obvious not to let you know when they are the enemy. If a woman studies a man she will know if he loves her. If she is too infatuated by him then she deceives herself. Then she becomes bitter. Everyone gets hurt because pain is a part of life but bitches allow pain to make them bitter. You can't allow yourself to fall victim to a bitch because she will never be satisfied. Because the problem is nothing you can solve but something she has to solve. All of my homegirls complain about the men they deal with but a lot of the problems are their fault. I had a good man we just weren't compatible so I didn't ever become bitter."

"So why do you come to visit me? If you know you and I aren't true love why do you come and spend intimate times with me?"

"I am just borrowing a good man until your soul mate claims you."

16
SOME THINGS NEVER CHANGE

Julani felt bad about that conversation he had with Shayla. Only because she had more hope in him finding his soul mate than he did. He didn't consider himself bitter but he didn't have a clue where to begin. He figured he would have to date and find out. Keeping his options open was definitely his intentions. I'm intelligent, educated, decent looking, I have a good job, why wouldn't I be able to find a good woman, he considered. Shayla saw a lot in him that he might not have seen in himself. But he would bide his time.

A couple of weeks after his conversation with Shayla he and Bruce went to the strip club. Bruce kept telling him about his ex-girlfriend Lisa working as a stripper. He had been hanging with Bruce a little more often because Jeff's marriage had consumed him. Every now and then he would be able to play basketball or bowling but nothing consistent. Bruce and Julani had a love hate relationship. It was times where Julani could have a good time with Bruce but other times he couldn't stand being in his presence. But since they had been hanging out a lot lately he grew fonder of Bruce. He could see a side of Bruce that Jeff always saw but he could never see. A kinder side that was more giving than expected.

They walked into the strip club and tried to find their way through the dim lights. Bruce walked straight to the bar to get a drink. Julani on the other hand sat near the stage because the girl on stage had a big ass. She was twirling around in her eight-inch heels like it was nothing. She was what Julani referred to as a redbone. She had a light complexion with light brown eyes. Her chest was damn near flat but she had a small waist and a real big booty. You could tell she thought that was her best asset because she made sure she gave you a good visual of it. She was hard in the face like she had been through a lot. Bruce came from the bar and handed Julani a beer.

"My treat dog." Bruce said while looking on stage.

"Good looking out!"

There were some good-looking women half naked walking around all over the place. Julani had been to a strip club before but he didn't like to go. He hated that he could grind but couldn't bust the nut. Paying someone for blue balls didn't appeal to him too much. But he had to reconsider his thinking because there were women that he did like to see naked at this club. He sipped on his beer and relaxed while watching the performers. He'd forgotten why he had come in the first place.

"JULANI? Is that you?"

Julani started looking around nervously. Who in the hell is yelling my name in a strip club? He turned all the way around with his back to the stage. Standing in front of him was Lisa in a pink two-piece bikini and some matching six-inch heals.

"Boy I haven't seen you in years. How have you been?"

"I am doing fine what about you?"

"Shit I can't complain everything is the best it's gon' be. But you look good." Lisa eyed him up and down.

"Nothing has changed on you. You look just as attractive as I remember. Oh by the way this is my homeboy Bruce do you remember him?"

"He's been in here before and I thought he looked familiar but I couldn't put my finger on it. I never would have come up with that being your homeboy. I only remember Jeff."

"Well he just got married not too long ago. I was his best man." Julani proclaimed

"That's a trip because I didn't think he would ever get married." Lisa replied.

They both have a moment of silence. Julani had lied to her about her appearance. Her body still looked good but she had developed weed lips. She had that pretty chocolate complexion but those hard black weed lips made her look older than what she was. He was staring at her when Lisa broke the silence.

"Come over to the bar with me." She urged.

Julani followed her to the bar. Her ass was jiggling because she was experienced in teasing a man while she was half naked. She walked in the heels as if she had been walking in tennis shoes. No matter how bad her lips looked she still had a great looking ass Julani thought. She leaned over the bar.

"Ay Theresa get me two Long Island Ice Teas. Put it on my tab this is the nigga that broke my heart a long time ago. I ain't seen his fine ass since that day." She teased.

"Ay Lisa about that day. I am so sorry about how I did you. I really am not that kind of man. I wish I wouldn't have ever done you like that." Julani apologized. He made sure to give her eye contact to show his sincerity.

"Don't trip; we were both young and dumb. I was saying that because you were my first love that's all. Shit I don't even worry about that kind of stuff anymore." She dismissed the issue.

They both got their drinks. Julani felt obligated to drink it but since he was driving he didn't want to get drunk. So he sipped on it a little at a time while she downed hers. Now that she had alcohol in her she started walking over to him. She grinded her ass against his dick. She still knew how to arouse him like the old days. She clung on to him while Bruce was on the other side getting table dances. Lisa was practically giving him free table dances standing in front of him at the bar. Julani was eager to take her home that night but he had Bruce with him. He indicated to Bruce that it was time to go in sign language. He did it so that Lisa couldn't see him. If there wasn't going to be any sex tonight this needs to stop. Bruce walked over to the bar smiling from his table dances.

"You ready to go?"

"Yeah it is getting late." Julani said it as if it was Bruce's idea to leave.

"Well we should keep in touch. I stay out in Gardena now, we should hook up." She replied.

"That'll be cool, let me get your phone number."

Julani knew she wanted to hook up bad because she gave him her home and cell phone number. He smiled and opened his arms to give her a hug. When he put his arms around her she slid his hands down so that he could feel her ass.

"Is it as soft as you remember?" She whispered in his ear.

After a long and intimate hug Julani let her go so that he and Bruce could leave. Once they were outside Bruce started in.

"What do you mean it's getting late when it is only eleven o'clock? We could have stayed in there for another hour or so. You seen that redbone with the big ole ass I was dancing with? Man she had ass." Bruce complained.

"Yeah but Lisa was getting me hot and I knew that I wasn't going to hit tonight."

"Yeah, but its Saturday night and we are going in kind of early for the weekend. You got an idea of somewhere else we can go."

"Not off hand but let me stop and get some gas at this Arco." Julani replied.

They pulled up with the music playing loud. Bruce handed Julani ten dollars for gas as he was getting out to pay the clerk. Julani just bought himself a truck so it took about forty-five dollars to fill his tank. He quickly paid the clerk then walked back to pump the gas.

"Damn, this thing doesn't want to work." A distraught female voice said.

Julani glanced over on the other side of the gas pump. He saw an attractive woman having problems with her pump. He put his gentleman charm in full gear.

"Let me help you with that." Julani smoothly suggested.

"Why thank you. There are not enough gentlemen in the world today." She smiled.

"How are you doing my name is Julani?" Julani extended his hand.

"My name is Charlene." She smiled again.

"What is a beautiful young woman doing out this late by herself?"

"Oh, I just came from a friend's party. I didn't want to stay up all night so I left early. What is a handsome Black man doing out this late on a Saturday night?" She shot back at him.

"Well thank you for the compliment but my buddy and I went to a club and decided to leave early also. If you are available we should go out sometime."

"If I'm available some time? Even if I weren't available you would probably want to go out 'some time." She chuckled.

"I try to respect another man's territory even though many men don't respect that code, I try to."

"Either you do or you don't. Try means that you have slipped up a few times." She smiled. She was definitely testing his wit.

"Well not so far but I don't know what the future holds."

"At least you're honest. Here is my number."

She gave Julani the number as he inserted it into his cell phone. Charlene looked at him to see if he would give her serious eye contact. When Julani looked up from his phone he looked her right in her eye.

"What?" Julani asked while smiling.

"Nothing, I just wanted to see if you would give me eye contact that's all."

"What's that about?"

"One guy I dated was a compulsive liar but you knew when he was lying because he would never look you in the eyes. It is just something that I measure men by."

Julani didn't like what he heard. But she was so fine that he overlooked her information overkill. He smiled at her and simply said.

"Well I don't have to lie to you because you are not my wife." Julani joked.

"Are you married? Or are you involved?" She asked as if she just remembered.

"No not at all but I know that men lie to their wives to keep peace at home so it was a little joke."

She laughed and he waved goodbye as she jumped in her car. Julani felt the tension immediately but his attraction to her was too strong so he ignored it. He jumped in the car after filling his tank.

"So did you get that fine ass girl's number?" Bruce asked as soon as he got inside the car.

"Sure did! Her name is Charlene."

"I seen her fine ass when she pulled up. She looks like she's high maintenance."

"Yeah she did seem like she was a little high strung. She could have figured out how to pump that gas herself. She saw some guys and cried lady in distress. But I didn't mind and she was cool enough to slide me the number." Julani replied.

The next day Julani called Lisa and Charlene. He set up a date with Charlene for the following Saturday. Lisa would come by that night. It was Sunday and she didn't have to go to work. Julani had to go to work in the morning so he had her stop through around nine in the evening. She came over with a tight fitted nylon dress with matching pumps. She had her hair in a bun and covered her weed lips with pretty burgundy lipstick. She smiled as she entered his two-bedroom apartment.

"Damn Julani this place is better than mine! Do you mind if I look around?"

"Go right ahead and make yourself at home."

She quickly took off her pumps and laid them on the side of the couch. She explored every aspect of his apartment going in his computer room and bedroom. She was really enjoying the way he had his place laid out.

"You are really doing well for yourself. I always knew that you would make something of yourself." Lisa smiled.

Julani was bewildered at how flattered she was about his apartment. In Julani's opinion he felt that it was about time he bought a house. But she acted as if he was filthy rich and living in a mansion. It let Julani know that her mind was still in the ghetto. She hadn't learned to try to expand her mind beyond the environment she grew up in.

"Would you like something to drink?" He asked. He was attempting to think positive.

"Yeah, that will be fine."

"Lisa I know you make good money dancing?" He asked.

"Most nights are good but some nights are slow. Quick money goes just as fast as it comes in. Stripping is like the dope game for females. It is a whole bunch of highs and lows. I might get out of dancing in another two years."

"Are you tired of it?"

"Yeah, I have been putting away a little money so that I can go to school. I want to be an X-Ray Technician. I heard they pay pretty good money. Something normal other than these niggas feeling on me for ten lousy ass dollars."

"Girl I know you will work it out." Julani sat down while handing her a drink.

"That is the same thing you did when you first met me. You sat down next to me then handed me a drink. I remember that shit like it was yesterday." She remarked.

"I remember it too." Julani whispered.

He leaned over and started kissing her. She sat her drink down as they begun French kissing on the couch. Julani slid his hands right down to her ass. Then slides her dress off and realized she doesn't have on any panties. He stuck his finger in her pussy as she moaned. Julani knew what she came over for. So he was going to give her what she wanted. She slid the dress over her head and started sucking on her titties. Now Julani was hard as a rock. He got up to take off his clothes. She was already butt naked standing in front of him. He pulled a condom from out of his pocket. He slid the condom on and she got on top. She was bouncing up and down on his dick.

"You knew you was gon' get this pussy huh Julani. You know this is your pussy huh." She moaned.

"Yeah baby, my pussy." Julani whispered back.

He had her ride him until she came. Then he got up and bent her over the couch. Julani had been saving his nut so that he could do it to her doggy style. He quickly plunged into her without mercy or restraint. It has been a long time but that big ole ass still was soft and jiggely. He got more excited as she pushed her ass into his pelvis.

"Give it to me hard baby. I missed yo dick so much." She moaned.

This turned Julani on more. He started going faster and faster. He spread her ass cheeks and gripped each one firmly. He pushed harder and harder. Harder and harder he pushed. Then suddenly he collapsed.

"Oh shit, this feels so good." He moaned.

"You like it baby? It's yours." She whined.

Julani pulled out the condom filled with his semen. He stood about a foot away from her trying to catch his breath. He peeled the condom off, walked in the bathroom and flushed it down the toilet. When he came back into the living room Lisa was sitting on the couch.

"You got a washcloth?" She asked.

"Yeah in that hallway closet."

She went into the closet then walked into the restroom. While the water was running she talked over the noise.

"Would it be cool if I spent the night?"

"Well I get up to go to work at seven so that might not be a good idea. I know your hours don't have you getting up that early."

"Yeah that's true." She agreed.

17
REAL LOVE

This was the third time Lisa had called today. She kept calling as if she didn't have anything else to do. Julani was frustrated but he didn't have a solution. He finally picked up the phone when she called for the fourth time.

"Hello!"

"Julani, this is Lisa!"

"I know who this is! How many times have you called today?"

"I don't know maybe twice!"

"The caller ID got you down for calling four times. What's up with that?"

"I don't know but I miss you." She whined.

"You just seen me Sunday it is only Tuesday." Julani fired back.

"Yeah, but seeing you Sunday brought back some old memories that's all. When can I see you again?"

"I don't know."

"How about Saturday?" She insisted.

"I am supposed to do something with Jeff and Bruce Saturday night." Julani lied. Saturday was the night he was going on a date with Charlene.

"Well maybe Sunday again. You know I could come visit you before I go to work. How about I come by tomorrow?" She persisted.

Julani paused before answering. His mind was telling him to say no. But his dick was telling him to say yes.

"Well what time are you talking about coming through? It can't be too late." Julani finally asked.

"I was thinking around seven. I don't have to be on stage until nine-thirty anyway."

"Okay that's cool." He listened to his dick.

The next night Lisa called around six-thirty in the evening. He let her know that it was okay to come through. She was over his house in twenty minutes. The number was blocked but since he wasn't dodging anyone he went ahead and answered it. She was close to the area Julani thought. He let her inside and sat back down on the couch. She had a large Gucci bag that she was carrying. She had on a tight brown blouse, a jean mini-skirt and brown sandals with the high arch heels. Julani glanced at her and he thought she looked good. He was somewhat distracted by something on the news. Lisa thought she dressed cute for him and was disappointed about how nonchalant he was about it. She asked him if she could use his restroom.

She came out of the restroom smiling from ear to ear. The news piece he was watching was over so she had his undivided attention.

"What are you grinning about?"

"I was hoping that Sunday wasn't a one night stand. I am just happy to see you." She replied.

"I am happy to see you too. Come here."

Julani wasted no time. She walked over to him with her finger in her mouth like a little child. She stood in front of him still smiling. He started rubbing on her thick legs. He lifted her mini-skirt up and once again she didn't have on panties. He rubbed on her soft ass while she stood still in front of him. Julani was getting extremely horny playing with her big ole booty. He unzipped her mini-skirt and it slid right off. She took off her blouse. Now she didn't have any clothes on. Julani had on his short set so that it would be easy access. He slid his shorts off with ease and pulled her down to her knees.

She grabbed a hold of his manhood and began sucking. She had definitely improved since they were teenagers. She was showing that her being in the sex industry had improved her oral performance. She was giving him head like she was trying to get him sprung. When she finally stopped he stood her back up. He bent her over while she was still standing up. He told her to grab her ankles. She quickly complied. He hurriedly put on the condom. He then rubbed his dick against her clitoris. Then he plunged inside of her without warning. She shrieked from the sudden penetration. He was always ruff with Lisa. He put one of his legs on the couch then pulled her closer. He was going deep inside of her with fast merciless strokes. It was the type of pleasure pain that she had grown to love. Most men that she had dated want to ravage her in the doggy style position. But Julani was different she thought because he was her first love. This was pure unadulterated sex to Julani, nothing more nothing less.

Julani couldn't fathom himself being with a stripper. Especially an ex-girlfriend who only gave him sex the last time they were together. But Julani had no problem giving her the high hard one. She acted as if that was all she wanted anyway. As Julani was about to cum she started to jiggled her fat ass like she was riding the pole. This of course made him cum even harder. This time no one said anything. It was a simple hardcore fucking session. Julani threw off the condom and put on his shorts. She sat next to him on the couch. It was around seven-thirty by the time they were done.

"That's cool; I got another two hours to kick it." Lisa smiled.

Julani didn't say anything but in his mind he was like damn. He was hoping to get rid of her sooner than that.

"You think that you and I could ever get back serious again?"

"To tell you the truth, I am not ready for a serious relationship."

Translation was that she wasn't the kind of woman that Julani could see himself being with seriously. She was cool to have sex with but that was it. She rubbed on his chest. Since he had busted a nut everything she did at this point irritated him.

"Well let me know when you are ready because I am ready whenever you are."

"Nah I'm enjoying my freedom."

That Saturday Julani prepared for his date with Charlene. He made sure that he was looking sharp because he wanted to impress

"I told you we were just friends when you asked me about a relationship. Why are you making this so difficult?" He whispered loudly.

"Because all I am to you is a piece of ass. If you didn't want to get with me you shouldn't have stuck your dick in me."

Julani knew she was right about that. Especially now that he seen her making his life more difficult he really considered his action.

"You think the way you're acting now is a good reason for you to be my lady? Are you showing me that you want to be a good woman to me acting like that?" Julani lashed back.

"You weren't interested in me being your lady anyway nigga. Don't make it seem like you wanted us to hook up in the first place. All you were trying to do is fuck."

"Well we don't have to fuck anymore. Matter of fact you don't need to call me ever again." He spewed out with relief.

"Uh huh, talking about you is sorry for what you did to me. Looks like you the same nigga that dogged me years ago. You ain't changed you low down muthafucka. Yo dick is yo best friend just like any other nigga."

"Whatever!" Julani hung up the phone.

He walked back in to the dining area of the restaurant to see his food on the table. He apologized to Charlene who had a facial expression that was fierce. He had her sitting there alone for too long. Julani once again ignored another thing that irritated him. Julani tried to open up conversation with her but she gave him one-word answers. His cell phone started vibrating again. Charlene looked over at him with another cold stare as he silenced his phone. After the call again he just turned his phone off. He was secretly kicking himself for not cutting it off in the first place. Now he had to make the best of his awkward situation.

"I say we walk the promenade at Redondo Beach after dinner. We can talk and get to know each other."

"Maybe, if your little girlfriend doesn't keep calling." Charlene snapped.

"I don't have a girlfriend. Sometimes people get the wrong impression that's all." Julani explained.

"Whom are you referring to when you say people?"

"No one you know."

"Well the way she is calling appears to be a woman you had sex with. Are you another one of those hit it and quit it brothers." Charlene sharply asked.

"What I did before me and you hooked up is irrelevant. What you should worry about is how I treat you."

"Well excuse the hell out of me. Your phone rings a thousand times and you don't expect me to say anything?" She whispered loudly.

"We don't have to argue about this let us enjoy our meal and have a good time. The person that was on the phone is of no concern to you trust me."

"We'll see, that might be a pattern that may continue with me; then it will be a concern of mine."

"Trust me; you are two totally different people. What do you say we go to Redondo Beach Pier after dinner?"

"It depends on how I feel." She replied.

Julani was a little pissed off after she said that. He felt that she was quick to jump the gun without knowing all the details. Now she had an attitude because he received a few phone calls. Julani wanted to walk out the door then but he kept his cool. The spread at the Velvet Turtle was fabulous. He enjoyed the meal but he was growing wary of his companion. After the meal he wanted to take her straight home. He started towards the direction to take her home.

"I thought we were going to Redondo Beach?" She finally broke her silence.

"Well you never said yes or no so I assumed you didn't want to go. It isn't like you've been talking to me."

"Well fine you can take me home." She pouted.

Julani continued to go in the same direction heading to her house. He was really irritated by her at this point. He couldn't wait to get her to her door safely so he could leave the uncomfortable situation. He tried to get to her apartment in record speed. He pulled up and opened the door for her. Then walked her to the doorsteps. She stood there without saying anything. When Julani looked at her he realized that she was very beautiful from a physical standpoint. He couldn't stand her attitude on this first date though.

"Well I apologize for the incessant phone calls I think that we could have had a better date without them."

"You are telling the truth about that." Charlene rolled her eyes.

"But you didn't have to take it that way either." Julani replied.

"Well how was I supposed to take it? You are on a date with me, and someone, probably another bitch, couldn't stop calling. To me that was rude, insensitive and inconsiderate. It lacks taste and class." She scolded.

"So now I don't have any class because I forgot to cut my phone off. Let us end the date with you insulting…"

Suddenly a very attractive woman walked toward the door in between the both of them.

"Excuse me."

She was a beautiful woman with beautiful smooth caramel skin. She had a mole right above her lip. She was just as attractive as Charlene but she had humility about herself. Where Charlene was arrogant she was humble. She probably would have been a better date than Charlene, he considered.

"What is going on Stephanie, this is my date Julani." Charlene said.

"Nice to meet you." Julani extended his hand.

She shook his hand and gave him brief eye contact. Then she walked into the apartment. Julani then turned his attention back to Charlene.

"Take care of yourself Charlene." He replied while walking away.

While driving home he felt bitter. His date was sabotaged because of a woman he was having sex with. Will real love always take a back seat to his sexual drive? He had already admitted that he had a problem the question now was how to cure the problem.

18
THE HELPMEET

"Why in the fuck you keep calling me? We had sex twice and now I am supposed to commit myself to you." Julani snarled.

"I just want you to give me a little attention and you are acting like a muthafuckin dog." Lisa snapped

"You are a stripper Lisa. How am I supposed to act when you are rubbing on different niggas' dicks every night? For ten dollars a dance."

"So because I'm a stripper bitch I ain't worthy to be your lady?" She asked. He had already offended her from the first comment.

"You know the difference between a bitch and a hoe. A hoe fucks everybody and a bitch fucks everybody but me. You grind on every nigga in the club so what does that make you."

"Huh, what?" She was briefly dumbfounded.

"Oh so now you don't understand. Do you know the difference between a dumb bitch and a stupid bitch? A stupid bitch does dumb shit and a dumb bitch can't comprehend. You can't comprehend so you a dumb bitch." Julani viciously insulted her.

"If my cousins weren't in prison I would tell them to beat yo ass." Lisa screamed into the phone.

Julani hung up the phone. Lisa had been getting on his nerves leaving stalker messages. He couldn't take it after awhile so he finally answered the phone. He remembered being told that all pussy ain't good pussy. You would think that he would have learned from the Jamaican girl but he still hadn't learned. A hard head makes a soft ass.

He was too ashamed to call his mother so he called Jeff. By this time Jeff wanted to get out the house for a little while. He stopped by to check up on Julani. Julani played ten messages Lisa left on his answering machine.

139

"What you need to do is file a restraining order." Jeff said while grabbing a Heineken from the refrigerator.

"You think it's that serious. She hasn't been popping up at my house or anything but she has been calling a lot."

"Yeah Lani, if you don't do it now it may get worse. Then it will be too late for you to do anything. I remember her cousin Lanette being a little possessive but not anything like this."

"Yeah, I will have to do it after I get off work tomorrow. You want to shoot up to the pool hall and pick up a few games?" Julani asked. He figured playing pool would take his mind off of Lisa.

"Why not?"

They went up to the pool hall and there were women everywhere. It was unusually crowded tonight but they were able to secure a table. While Julani and Jeff shot pool a couple of girls were playing across from them. Julani noticed a pretty dark skin dime piece giving him the eye. After he beat Jeff in the first game he walked over there to talk to her. She definitely fit his preference with a big ole booty and skintight jeans. Julani talked to her for a brief moment and then asked her for her number. She gave him the number with no hesitation. Her name was Krystal.

"My friend is digging your homeboy, what is up with him." Krystal asked

Julani knew the right thing to say. But before he was called a cock blocker he looked over at Jeff with a sly grin. Jeff knew what that meant and pointed at his wedding band.

"My homeboy is happily married." Julani replied.

"So what about you are you married too?" Krystal asked.

"No not yet. When the time comes it will happen but I'm not rushing into anything." Julani walked back to his pool table.

"Well call me and we can kick it."

"Okay!"

Julani walked over to the pool table smiling from ear to ear. He slid the phone number into his pocket.

"Ay man I didn't mean any disrespect concerning your marriage but I had to get a confirmation or I would look like a…"

140

"Cock blocker! I know you don't mean any disrespect; I didn't even take it that way. But you are definitely disrespecting yourself. I don't know Lani you really ain't looking for a winner." Jeff sounded disappointed.

"What are you talking about Jeff she was fine as hell? Then she got that big ole ass. If you were single you telling me you wouldn't hit." Julani asked.

"But look how she carries herself. That's all she can be to you is a piece of ass. You can get that from Shayla. Why mess with a female that you know ain't nothing but trouble. She was bending over in those tight jeans trying to show her best asset to the world. She doesn't have any shame to her game. You can do better than that."

"Well everyone is not able to pull a winner like Sherise, homeboy. I work with the scraps that I'm given." Julani replied. There was a hint of irritation in his tone and Jeff felt it.

"Come on dog, you gotta think better of yourself than that? I've known you all my life and I don't know a better brother. You need a woman that will help you be the man that you are striving to be. I mean mentally, spiritually and emotionally becoming strong with the help of a good woman. You feel me?" Jeff explained

"Yeah I feel you, but it is hard to find a woman like that. If she is strong she wants to run your life for you. If she is weak than all she is going to do is tear down your life. I am starting to believe that I don't know how to pick a good woman. Yeah I could get some unattractive woman that is good in all those areas you mentioned but I'll always want to fuck someone else." He replied.

They both start laughing. Julani agreed with Jeff on the inside but at this point in his life he felt helpless.

The next day he decided to have lunch in his plaza suite cafeteria. His buddy from work had called in sick so he was rolling solo today. He didn't want to go too far; but to get out the office he went to eat at the tables outside. He ordered his food from the cafeteria and enjoyed the warm weather. As he sat down he noticed a pretty young woman. He had to glance again because she looked familiar. He couldn't put his finger on it. He chose to ignore what he saw. About twenty minutes into his lunch she got up from her table. She was deep in thought as she walked away. When she walked passed his table she gave him a quick glance and smiled. Then she did a double take as though he looked familiar to her as well. She also ignored her feeling and kept walking.

That following Monday Julani and his buddy Matt agreed to go to the cafeteria. It was always more convenient to go the cafeteria but since they were given two hours for lunch they tried to get out of the building. Julani ordered a turkey sandwich on rye bread with a pickle, Matt ordered the same then they sat down to eat. Twenty minutes into their lunch the same girl came walking outside to sit at one of the tables. She was very attractive and carried herself with class. But Julani was going crazy trying to figure out where he knew her.

"So that is why you wanted to eat in the cafeteria today, dude. She is beautiful" Matt noticed her.

Julani laughed and continued to eat. He kept glancing over at her hoping that she would look up and give eye contact. She gave him none. She was too engulfed in what she was doing. She appeared to be reading a novel. Julani finally built up enough courage to walk over to her.

"Excuse me, I know this may sound like a pick up line but you look familiar. Like I have seen you somewhere before." He smiled.

"You are familiar to me as well. But I can't put my finger on it; I assumed that I have seen you here but my thoughts suggests that is has been elsewhere." The young woman replied.

"My name is Julani, Julani Jasper and I live in Long Beach."

"I've heard that name once or twice. My name is Stephanie Miller." She sat her book down then stood up to shake his hand.

Julani suddenly remembered where he knew her. He didn't want to let her know that he had suddenly remembered. He just went along with the conversation.

"Do you work somewhere in this building?" Julani asked.

"Yes I do, I work for FOX Television technical support. I just began three months ago." Stephanie replied.

"That's wonderful, I work for FOX also but I am a communications analyst. It has been going on two years since I've been here. Do you always go to lunch down here?"

"Well, lately while the weather is good I try to get some sunshine for being in an office all day. The cafeteria is convenient and I can come outside to eat so it fits me just fine."

"Well I see that you are reading 'The Coldest Winter Ever' by Sistah Souljah. Is it good?"

"Very good so far. I can't seem to put it down. I'll probably finish it by the end of this week." Stephanie smiled.

"Well I will leave you to your reading. I look forward to talking to you again."

"The feeling is mutual Mr. Jasper." Stephanie blushed.

From that day forward Julani took his lunch in the cafeteria. He would anticipate seeing Stephanie. Every time he saw her he would try to get deeper into his conversations with her. Julani loved how much she kept her face in a book. She was an adamant reader. One week it was The Coldest Winter Ever. After that it was The Purpose Driven Life, Mis-education of the Negro, Waiting to Exhale, The Autobiography of Malcolm X. He couldn't believe how much she read. It was inspiring. His days were filled with him counting the hours when he could to talk to Stephanie again. She was extremely beautiful in mind, body and spirit. She carried herself like a woman of dignity and class. After three weeks of meeting her in the cafeteria he finally built up the courage to ask her out.

"I don't know Julani, where would we go?" She sounded doubtful.

"I was thinking a dinner somewhere nice."

"How about this, instead we meet at IHOP at nine o' clock Sunday morning." She gave him a sly smile.

He agreed even though Sunday was the mornings he loved to sleep in. He had to spend time with her outside of the job. It was something about her that fascinated him. He was hoping that she never caught on that he dated her roommate. He kept reminding himself that he must remain optimistic. Stephanie had a deepness that he hadn't seen in many women. She was as exotic as Naomi

Campbell. She was a wake up in the morning beautiful like Toni Braxton. Her womanly strength and power had a quiet resolve as Jada Pinkett Smith. She had a royal disposition like Angela Bassett. She had a spiritual feel like Jill Scott. In fact whenever he thought of Stephanie he thought of that Jill Scott song 'A Long Walk'. He was extremely infatuated. He wanted to see what she was all about. Even though she was extremely sexy he wasn't clouded by sex. She made him open his mind to other things.

Sunday morning came around. She told Julani to dress conservatively casual. He threw on a nice button up shirt with matching slacks. Instead of dress shoes he wore some comfortable loafers made by Gucci. When he pulled up she was standing outside her car, he was ten minutes early. She had on beige matching two-piece with brown sandals. They hugged each other since it was away from the work plaza suite. They both sat down to have a nice breakfast. They laughed and talked as time flew by. Stephanie was definitely more comfortable outside of work. They could talk about a vast amount of subjects because they were both well read. To Julani it was like talking to his best friend. About an hour later he noticed Stephanie looking at her watch. He ignored it the first time. But after she did it a couple of more times he spoke up.

"Do you have to be somewhere?"

"Well, to be honest I was hoping you and I could go somewhere together." She replied.

Just like Julani thought she was one of those religious fanatics. He shrugged while anticipating her suggestion.

"I want to take you to this religious service."

I knew it, I knew it; Julani thought.

"I don't usually go to this church but a friend of mine suggested that I check it out because it might be an interesting subject the preacher might have today." She explained.

"Have you ever been to this church before?" Julani asked.

"No not at all. But my girlfriend told me that this Jamaican Preacher will be their guest speaker and she told me he was powerful. So I told her I would try to check it out." She explained.

144

He felt much more comfortable since she had never been herself. He escorted her out the door then they drove in his car. It wasn't that far from the IHOP they were eating so it took fifteen to twenty minutes.

"You had this all planned out huh." Julani asked.

"Sort of, don't be mad at me."

"I'm not mad, I was concerned at first until you told me you had never been yourself."

"Yeah, this is my first time too. So I don't know what to expect."

When they walked in the church Julani scanned the room. He thought that they might both be dressed too casual. But he noticed that they weren't the only ones dressed casual. It was that kind of environment. Shortly after they sat down the Keynote Preacher was introduced. His subject manner was marriage and the helpmeet. He dealt with how a man and a woman were supposed to work toward a union with God. He said that a husband or wife is supposed to help each other fulfill their purpose to God. A helpmeet he continued was intended for him or her to help you meet the destiny you were born to do. A man and woman are the two halves of one being. The Preacher went on to explain that marriage was half of faith and neither man nor woman is complete without the other. Julani was dumbfounded. These principles stayed stuck in his head.

Julani pulled up next to Stephanie's car after the service and sat there for a moment. Both were in deep thought so the drive back was quiet. Julani escorted her to her car then gave her another hug. This time she offered Julani her cell phone number. He thanked her then hugged her again. When he made it home he felt invigorated. He walked over to his answering machine and there were only two messages. His Mother and Jeff were the only calls. Lisa hadn't called in four days. He had filed the restraining order but chose not to enforce it. Now he felt better, now he felt good.

19
CAUSE AND EFFECT

Early Tuesday morning Julani came outside to see his two front tires were flat. He had to call in late waiting for Triple A. How could both his tires be on a flat by the morning? When he came home the night before his tires were fine. It was too fishy for him. He smelled a rat. After not hearing from Lisa in six days he assumed that she had caught the hint. He should have known better. The last time she talked to him she was still fumed about him calling her a dumb bitch. Her mentality was clear, he wasn't going to just fuck her then dump her like before. She felt like he owed her something. Julani felt like that was the thinking of a whore. What did he expect if she was grinding on men for money? He also had to consider that all strippers don't act like Lisa. There was something going wrong in her head personally. But he worried about having to look at himself as well. What did he do to deserve this? He had a lot on his mind on his way to work… running late. This was a dilemma that he was going to have to solve quickly.

When he got to work everyone was already in motion. He hated showing up late when everything was moving. He liked starting when everyone else started so he could know what was going on. Matt didn't have a problem with bringing him up to speed. But it was also the principle; he dealt with a lot of corporate white people. He was a proud Black man and he didn't want to misrepresent his people. First thing someone would say was that Black people always have excuses. That was the first time he was ever late so he swallowed it. He just didn't want it to happen again.

Lunchtime came and he met Stephanie down at the cafeteria just like the day before. She was just as eager to see him, as he was to see her. She smiled when he came walking through the cafeteria door. She was already in line about to pay for her food.

146

"I didn't think you were showing up today. I ran down to my car and didn't see your truck. I know you get in an hour earlier than I do so I didn't expect to see you at lunch." Stephanie smiled.

"I was running a little late. Something unexpected happened." Julani said grabbing something quick to eat.

They walked outside after Julani paid for his food. They sat at the same table they always sat. Since Julani had two hours for lunch and Stephanie had one he spent his first hour with her.

"Was everything okay? Nothing too bad this morning was it?" Stephanie asked.

"Can I be honest with you?" Julani asked.

"Sure!"

"I have a woman stalking me. She was an ex-girlfriend from a long time ago and we linked back up. She wanted it to be a serious relationship but I am not interested in her like that. I am not sure if she flattened my tires but I can't think of anyone else that would do that to me. I put out a restraining order but I haven't caught her in the act. I bet you think I am another brother with drama." He replied.

"No not really. At least you were honest. Is that the same girl that kept calling you when you were on your date with Charlene?" She asked.

Julani dropped his jaw. He couldn't believe she remembered.

"Yeah, actually that is who kept calling. When did you know that you knew me from dating Charlene? You know we only went out once?" He muttered.

"The next day I knew. I brought your name up to her that next night and she reminded me that you were the guy at the door that night I came home late. She had me describe you and the truck you drive. That is when she told me about the girl that kept calling on the date."

"You probably look at me in a bad way after Charlene was through with me?" He leaned in and half-heartedly smiled.

"No not really. I wouldn't be eating lunch with you everyday if I thought badly of you." She dismissed the notion with her hand.

From that day forward they would spend lunch together. Julani liked everything about her especially how she was his friend also. They even were comfortable about old relationships. What they could have done better and what drama a relationship brought. For weeks Stephanie was a hot item.

He finally kissed her three weeks into dating. They were walking to the car in the parking lot of 'The Block' in Orange County. He opened up the car door to let her in and her body grazed his. He seized the moment and grabbed her by the waist. She looked at him in his eyes as Julani hesitated. Then they finally kissed. Julani didn't want to let her go. The kiss was passionate and refreshing. It was extremely intimate without being over sexual. He wanted Stephanie as his woman. She wanted him as her man. Julani hadn't felt this good about a woman in years. He took her home and drove home feeling content.

When he went to his apartment he noticed that his window was busted out. How could a wonderful day end like this? He called the manager about the broken window. The on-sight manager told him he had heard the noise of broken glass but assumed it was a bottle. Julani was troubled but he had a certain amount of peace in his heart. He decided to call up Stephanie. She had just gotten in her bed. She wasn't expecting him to call until tomorrow.

"What's going on Julani? I wasn't expecting you to call until tomorrow.'

"Would you believe that Lisa broke out a window in my apartment? I don't know what to do about this because she is sneaky enough not to be seen. I will go crazy if she keeps this up."

"Don't go crazy. Don't allow Lisa to kill your spirit. She wants you to feel like she feels. Bitter! Don't feed into that what goes around comes around."

"Well maybe I wronged her for being with her knowing that I didn't want to be with her as a couple. I have to face the wrong I did, you know what I mean Stephanie. This could have been avoided."

"Well you are dealing with your Karma right now. But it doesn't have to consume you. A woman's natural inclination is to feel you are committed to her after you sleep with her. Her innate nature demands that a man when taking her body willingly takes the responsibility of what come with it. That is why women should be sure he wants to commit before they give a man their body. Lisa doesn't know how to express her nature. But she definitely feels you are obligated. Her emotional instability has caused her to vandalize your things. Repay her viciousness with kindness and see how she reacts." Stephanie explained.

"Repay it with kindness? I don't know about that she is causing me a lot of trouble."

"Just try it Julani. You have already admitted that you are somewhat responsible for this Karma coming back on you. You will catch her off guard if you repay her with kindness."

Julani thought long and hard about what Stephanie told him. Stephanie definitely made him want to be better. But what could he do in kindness that can be heartfelt. That next morning he decided to go to the flower shop. Then he stopped at Sees Candy. He sat down afterwards and hand wrote a two-page letter to Lisa. He explained how he shouldn't have called her a dumb bitch. He let her know that he wanted to seriously repent for what he did. He poured every emotion concerning Lisa into that letter so that she would know that it was sincere. He also explained to her that true repentance is not only in words but also in action.

His eyes watered up when he finished the letter. He had admitted his weakness to sex and wanted to overcome it. He knew he had a problem and he was telling that to Lisa. He knew that she didn't work on Sundays so he waited until Monday night to go up to the club. When he got up there the guy at the door looked at him like he was crazy. He explained that he had brought a present for the dancer called Luscious. The security guard reluctantly let him in. He sat down in the corner away from the stage. When he looked on stage the girl wasn't Lisa. He patiently waited until he seen Lisa walk out in a turquoise two-piece bikini and six inch stiletto heels switching like she owned the world. When she saw Julani she stopped in her tracks. She gave him a look that pierced right through him.

"What the fuck is you doing here? What you fucking another bitch up here?" She snapped.

"No, the flowers and candy are for you. I also wrote this letter to apologize for how I have been acting."

"So you miss this pussy huh?" She said with self-gratification.

Julani ignored her comment and handed her the flowers and candy. She smelled the flowers and breathed a sigh of content. Another dancer walked by with a slimmer build seeing what Julani had brought Lisa.

" Bitch you got it going on when you got niggas coming up here with flowers and candy for yo ass. Go ahead make them sprung."

Lisa just smiled back at the girl without responding. She felt good about him bringing her flowers. Her pride had been fed. She glanced at the envelope and opened the letter. Some guy was trying to get her attention for a table dance but she ignored him. When she finished reading the letter her eyes welled up and she gave Julani a hug.

"I'm sorry for being fucked up toward you Julani, you just hurt me boo. I thought that we would have made a good couple. But you are right we do have too much bad history to start from scratch. I guess all I wanted from you was a little attention." She confessed.

Julani didn't have anything else to say. He felt good about repenting. He felt like he had a monkey on his back that he had been trying to rid himself of. He kissed her hand goodbye and walked out the club. He had to look at the cause of his problems. When he paid close attention he could tell that he had it coming. From Tammy that was able to manipulate him with sex. To Malika giving him a venereal disease. Every woman that he dealt with revolved around sex. So then he had to deal with a woman that made a living off of sex. She put worth on what she gave him in a way that forced him to think. By vandalizing his apartment and flattening his tires she was determined to make him pay one way or another.

Julani woke up the next morning thinking about what he had done. His outlook on life was better because he wasn't burdened. He had a woman in his life that gave him hope. He addressed a potentially violent situation with flowers and candy. The old honey is better than vinegar concept of thinking. He and Stephanie were spending as much time as they could together. This was her last week with FOX Television. Her company had completed their task for the company and was now moving to help another company with technical support. So they took full advantage of all the time they spent together.

Julani knew that he was falling for Stephanie. His mother was throwing a barbecue and he decided to invite her. Julani only had three girlfriends that met his mother. Deidre, Lisa and Tammy were the only three that formerly met her. By this time he had dozens of sex partners but those were the only three that he allowed to meet his mother. His mother always loved Deidre and would periodically ask about her. Lisa on the other hand was one his mother didn't like. Julani never told Lisa his mother disliked her. As for Tammy, his mother thought she was nice she just didn't like the way Tammy kissed up to her. This made her not trust Tammy.

Saturday afternoon was the day of the barbecue. Julani was more nervous than a hooker in church. He appeared to be more nervous than Stephanie. But Stephanie was always cool as ice. She didn't let that much get to her. He also invited Jeff and Sherise who would meet him there. He hadn't introduced Stephanie to them either. Julani showed up a little early to help his mother out any way he could. He found his mother in the backyard putting seasoning on the meat.

"What's going on mama, how is everything cooking?"

"Good baby!"

Julani hugged and kissed her on the cheek.

"Mama this is Stephanie."

His mother turned around to greet Stephanie. Instantly his mother thought that she was beautiful. She hugged her and smiled.

"He knows me as mama, but girl you can call me Debra. Julani go grab me that barbecue sauce cooking on the stove. Watch it now because it's hot."

Julani walked in the kitchen and stirred the sauce. As he was stirring the doorbell rang. He cut off the stove to answer the door. Lo and behold it was Jeff and Sherise showing up early. Sherise was about four and a half months pregnant and beginning to show. He hugged both of them. Sherise quickly took a seat on the couch. Julani and Jeff started shooting the shit. They found themselves talking about all kinds of things.

"Julani, did you forget that I need to put barbecue sauce on the chicken in order for it to be barbecue chicken." His mother yelled from outside.

Julani quickly jumped up to rush the barbecue sauce to his mother. When he got outside he handed the barbecue sauce to his mother.

"I don't know what I am going to do with you boy." Debra remarked.

"Sorry about that mama. Jeff and Sherise are inside and me and Jeff got carried away."

"I need to see Sherise; she is probably showing right now. What is she, five or six months pregnant now?" Debra asked.

"I think she is almost five months. Stephanie could you come inside for a minute I have someone I would like you to meet."

Julani introduced her to Jeff and Sherise. Jeff's facial expression indicated that she was beautiful and he approved. Stephanie sat next to Sherise and they hit it off right away. He left Stephanie and Sherise to talk. Jeff was watching the game so Julani ran outside to help his mother. When he went outside his mother was finished putting the barbecue on one side of the chicken. She closed the barbecue grill while Julani was standing behind her. When she turned around he startled her.

"Boy, don't be sneaking up on me like that. Have you gone crazy?" Debra gasped.

Julani ignored her rhetorical question.

"So what do you think of her mama?" Julani eagerly asked.

"I like her, I like her a whole lot."

20
I DO

Six months passed for Stephanie and Julani. Their relationship was practically drama free. If they had a disagreement they were able to have a mature conversation to resolve the problem. They were the best of friends. Since she was at a different job now he had to see her after work. They would spend the day walking in the park nearby. Or they would cuddle up watching television. They both loved going down to the Santa Monica Promenade. They would buy Ice Cream and look in the different shops. Then they would spend hours in Barnes and Noble Bookstore. Julani couldn't ask for a better companion than Stephanie.

He realized that he more than loved her; he was in love with her. Both of their worlds revolved around each other. She was equally in love with him. They wanted to spend every waking moment with one another. It was a true romance at its pinnacle.

They both had nice apartments but Julani enjoyed being at her house. It was a predominantly black community so doing things in the neighborhood was pleasant. Charlene had moved out about a month before their six month mark. She was actually jealous of Stephanie and Julani's relationship. Stephanie asked Charlene would she mind her dating him. Charlene at the time didn't have a problem with it. Charlene thought her date with him was a disaster so she didn't care who he dated. But when she seen how well they clicked she grew envious. Instead of being out on her own Charlene decided to move back in with her parents. She referred to Stephanie as a man-stealing tramp. Stephanie was sweet but she wasn't a punk. She pulled Charlene's card and the tension made it obvious that someone would have to move out. Charlene chose to do so.

One day Julani came home from work eager to go to Stephanie's house. He had been spending the night over her house for the last two nights but now he needed a change of clothes. He ran in the house so he could grab clothes for a few days. Then he could meet Stephanie at her place. As he was getting everything ready someone banged on the door then rang the doorbell numerous times. Julani was annoyed. It was Friday night and he thought it might be his landlord. What could he want at six-fifty in the afternoon? Julani stopped what he was doing to answer the door. He swung the door open to quickly rid himself of the unwanted visitor.

"Oh so you thought you could buy a bitch off with some flowers, candy and a bullshit letter?" Lisa vindictively swayed her neck.

"Aw Lisa, I don't have time for this today, I'm headed somewhere." Julani said while trying to close the door on her.

"What, you going over to that bitch's house that you have been seeing. That bitch is pretty but she ain't built like me." Lisa snarled. She aggressively pushed herself inside.

Julani wouldn't budge from the door. Lisa knew that she wasn't stronger than him so she started kicking and swinging. Julani tried to restrain her while trying to keep the door from opening any further. It was practically impossible for him to do both. She was able to barge her way in the apartment. She quickly closed the door behind her.

"Lisa you need to leave before I call the police." Julani retorted.

"Come here Julani I know you miss me. Quit tripping and let's do what we always do when I come by to see you. This is yours whenever you want it. Come hit this ass." She whined.

"Not this time Lisa. Some things are more important than sex." Julani resisted.

"What that bitch got that I don't have?" Lisa persisted.

Julani wanted to say class but he held it in. Lisa had her hands all over him. He kept trying to head for the door. Finally he firmly grabbed her and put her outside of his house. She started swinging and screaming at the same time. He attempted to calm her down but to no avail. He tried to release her and go back into the house to call the police. He figured if she were locked out she would vandalize his car. Every time he tried to pull away she hung on for dear life. Either he was going to stay outside with her or she was coming in with him. The whole time she was still swinging and screaming. He pretended to get comfortable staying outside while she caught her breath. Then he quickly snatched off of her. She fell to the ground and he closed the door behind him.

Right when she hit the concrete the police pulled up. All they were able to see was Julani pushing her to the ground. They quickly jumped out the police car to come to her rescue.

"Ma'am are you okay?" One Police Officer asked.

The other Police Officer helped Lisa get up from off the ground.

"My boyfriend is tripping. I don't know what I'm going to do about him. He is breaking my heart." She complained.

The Police Officer that helped her up started banging on the door. Julani went into his room to call the police. When he heard the banging he brought the cordless into the living room.

"Lisa you better leave or the police are going to arrest you." He yelled through the door.

"Sir this *is* the police, can you step outside?"

Julani stood silent for a few seconds. How did they get here so fast when I haven't called them yet, Julani thought? Then it dawned on him that the neighbors probably called after hearing Lisa scream. He slowly opened the door and poked his head out.

"Yes officer can I help you."

"Sir we witnessed you assault this woman, can you step outside."

"No sir, she was assaulting me. She kept trying to get inside my house. What you witnessed was me trying to escape her grasp and she accidentally fell down."

"Baby why are you lying? You know that you have been dealing with this anger problem for some time now." Lisa replied.

So now the bitch is calm Julani thought.

"Sir we need you to step outside. You are under arrest. If we have to remove you from your home we will also charge you with resisting arrest." The Police Officer insisted.

"Okay I won't resist but if you arrest me I think you should arrest her as well. I have a restraining order on her and she can't prove that she lives here." Julani explained

"If you can show proof of your restraining order we will arrest her as well. But we witnessed you assault her so you have to go downtown with us."

Julani opened the door and let them in. They brought Lisa inside to detain her until he showed proof. He went into the kitchen and found it in his junk drawer. The Police Officer looked at the restraining order and they placed her under arrest. But since they saw him push her to the ground they arrested him as well. He was permitted to lock his door plus take his keys and wallet. Julani had never been to jail his entire life. He kept thinking to himself I thought I repented I thought I repented.

After booking and processing it was close to midnight. He was finally able to use a phone at the Long Beach Jailhouse. The first person he called was his mother. He told her everything that happened. She quickly got dressed in the middle of the night to bail her son out of jail. He didn't get released from jail until three in the morning.

He met a guy that was in a jail cell right next to him. The guy overheard the conversation he had with his mother.

"I couldn't help but overhear your conversation young brotha. Many times we have to suffer for the decisions we make concerning women. Next time you will probably choose your women more wisely."

"But sir, I repented and didn't try to be intimate with her anymore and I still end up in jail, it doesn't make sense."

"When you repent that doesn't mean that there are no repercussions. Sometimes we repent expecting repercussions to be given to us on our terms. But the Lord of the worlds decides what pain he wants you to endure. What lesson he wants to be taught. He either is teaching you to appreciate what you have or don't blow something good when you get it."

"I am now dating a beautiful woman and she is the joy of my life. I am ashamed to tell her what I just went through." Julani admitted.

"A real woman will understand that you had a debt that you owed and you are now paying it. You are probably suffering because you did something and you knew better but did it anyway. God will definitely spank you for that. If your current woman is the joy of your life then you attracted a queen because of the spirit you had. Learn from your experience and move on."

"I guess you're right. Before I got my act together and started facing my own weakness I was getting women with many different issues. This woman I am with helped me face my issues. She helped me become a better man." Julani proudly replied.

"Well when a man is connected to God he reflects God. A man that reflects God knows how to love a Black woman. On the other hand niggas will always attract bitches. And niggas and bitches don't know how to love each other right." The wise cellmate explained.

Julani pondered on what his cellmate said. It was profound in a simple way. Basically God loves Black women while Niggas Love Bitches. He had to go to jail to really understand that you get what you are. If you act like a nigga you will end up with bitches. Your aura will attract the people that carry the same mental and spiritual sicknesses that you carry. He was in a trance until an officer yelled in the cell.

"Jasper, first name, Julani, come to be processed for your release."

Julani eagerly jumped up to get released. When he made it to the cell door it dawned on him.

"Hey sir, if you don't mind me asking; what are you in here for?"

"It appears that I am in here to meet you." The cellmate smiled.

Julani smiled back and waved as he left with the officer. When he was finally released his mother was waiting in the car for him. He climbed in the car and hugged his mother. She drove off with the speed of light.

"I knew that girl wasn't right. But you probably had sex with her knowing you don't want to be with her huh?" She gave him an accusing eye.

"Yeah mama, I won't lie to you that is exactly what happened. I should have known better. A valuable lesson was learned for me today."

"Don't kick yourself too hard. Sometimes it takes that for us to wake up. Some things have to be taught the hard way."

His mother dropped him off at home and he immediately called Stephanie. He told her about everything and she understood. She even promised to go to court with him for his hearing. She was happy that he was safe.

"Baby why don't you come live with me. That way Lisa won't be able to find you."

Julani was flattered. He grabbed everything he needed to go to her house.

"Baby I will be there in half an hour." Julani rushed off the phone and out the door.

When he reached her door it was around five in the morning. The sun was just about to come out. The crack of dawn had begun when Stephanie opened the door.

"Will you marry me?" Julani said, bended on one knee with the platinum engagement ring in hand.

Stephanie started crying because it caught her totally off guard.

"Yes I will marry you. I love you so much."

Julani slipped the ring on her finger he had bought two days ago. He stood up and hugged her.

Eventually the charges against Julani were dropped because of his restraining order. Since Lisa didn't have proof that she lived at that residence she was put on strict probation. He didn't hold any ill will towards her but knew it was time to move forward. He had to reflect on his past relationships and ponder on what he could have done better. He definitely didn't want to make the same mistakes he made in the past with Stephanie. His ordeal with Lisa was definitely a fiery purification.

Six months later Stephanie and Julani had their wedding in the same church they had their first date.

"Will you take Julani Jasper to be your lawfully wedded husband? Through sickness and health, for richer or poorer till death do you part?"

"I do!"

"Will you take Stephanie Baker to be your lawfully wedded wife? Through sickness and health, for richer or poorer till death do you part?"

"I do!"

THE BEGINNING!!!

Part two:

GOD
LOVES
BLACKWOMEN
WHILE
NIGGAS
LOVE
BITCHES

NONFICTION

TABLE OF CONTENTS

1
INTRODUCTION

God Loves Black women while Niggas Love Bitches!
PaPa Sak

When I first wrote this book the intention was to make it a self help book. I later wondered about that. I'm figuring that it might be somewhat arrogant to assume that I know what is best for people in their relationships. There is no doubt that I've had my share of failed relationships. The original manuscript for the self help aspect was written years before I was married. After I was divorced I really considered it a waste of time to write this aspect of the book. I've recently reconsidered writing this part because truthfully there were some things I've learned that could possibly help others.

When a man is on a God level he is spiritually and morally sound. He doesn't try to justify wrong doing that he or someone else does. This doesn't suggest that he is under any particular religious doctrine. It just means that he's achieved a certain spiritual maturity that makes him pay attention to his self accusing spirit. This is a beautiful time in a man's life because he can sincerely strive to be better. In religious dogma people always point out the consequences to doing and being wrong. Many fanatics want to frighten men and women to be right. How about us looking at the beauty of being right? How about we point out the benefits in trying to live a good life?

We continually cheat ourselves out of what we deserve because we want to cheat at the rules of life. This world and this social order promote the lifestyle of corruption and shortcuts. We all have allowed ourselves to become purveyors of scandalous activities. Love is something that should really be examined for what it is. Love should be the goal of every human being but it has become tainted by underhanded thinking. In psalms 82 it points out that we are all gods. When you look at it from a deeper perspective you can see that since we were created in the image and likeness of God we can achieve a certain level of development. We don't have to dwell on the carnal aspect of life alone. We can reach spiritual heights that can give us the power and the beauty to overcome all obstacles in our path. This is the true understanding of 'Thy kingdom come, Thy will be done, on earth as it is in heaven'. We can do that with each relationship, one at a time. But we must first recognize the landmines that we place in front of ourselves.

We attract people of the opposite sex based upon the same traits we possess. The old saying of being equally yoked holds some relevance. It points out in one aspect how we attract what we are. If we act like niggas then we will definitely attract bitches. A nigga has a quality about him that shuns responsibility and obligation. He refuses to commit to someone or something because he doesn't want to deal with the burden. In the same token he attracts a woman that carries qualities that are similar but from a woman's perspective. He shuns his manly responsibilities and she shuns her womanly responsibilities then they both wonder why they don't have a healthy relationship. We will touch on these things in detail on each chapter with me pointing out my own experiences as well as my fictional character Julani. So sit back and contemplate these things because the objective is to learn and be better. This is not only for the reader to learn but for the writer to reflect on his mistakes as well. Maybe with a little help from the Most High we can get to the root of the problem.

Sincerely
PaPa Sak

2

THE PIMP AND WHORE GAME

Self-esteem is a handicap for my devilish goals
PaPa Sak

Can we truly obtain the beauty of love in the current mindset of our people? Is love just a myth that we have yet to grasp because of our behavior? Many of us have become victims of our own actions. We take for granted the beauty of love because every human being is entitled to it. Though this is true we still cannot obtain it if we don't follow certain principles. You know the saying; anything worth working for is worth having. Since we are in a world that expects everything to be instant we lack the work ethic to get what we deserve. The man eventually blames it on the woman and the woman blames it on the man. It is known as 'Sexual Politics'. When both sexes believe that there is a game to be played when interacting with the opposite sex. This is causing many relationships to become tainted and unhealthy. Since everyone is playing this deception game we tell lies to each other and ourselves. How about looking at failed past relationships for what they are? What brought about this bad result or this outcome that eventually hurt you? What could you have done better? Don't worry about for the time what your partner could have done better. Just pay attention to what you could have done better. We will get into the blame game later. First I want to us to pay attention to our own actions. Let's look at first how you could have avoided certain headaches even though your partner was mostly the blame. Let's do some self analysis.

In this analysis I want to first cover the topic of manhood. I won't get in full detail about manhood in this chapter but some things will be addressed to drive the point home. What is a man that doesn't want to work for what he deserves? He is a man of leisure. This is the term that pimps use when referring to themselves. We are not talking about pimps from a street point of view but from a moral point of view. I'm not referring to those that choose that profession. I'm referring to men that don't want to work towards a committed relationship but seek all the benefits that come with one. We are in a microwave fast paced world that makes everyone want things quick and fast. So this same mentality is implemented when interacting with the opposite sex. When one seeks true love he goes way beyond the surface. He works towards trying to get to know the person inside. He determines that a woman is worthy of him working towards being with her. But in a society of broken hearts and deceptive means, many of us are not willing to work towards that objective. We have become too bitter to trust someone enough to invest time, emotions and commitment to a person. So we settle for fast gratification which results in more hurt.

Many women follow the path of superficial in trying to attract the opposite sex. Women offer what they believe men want. It is very natural for a man to want sex but a sincere real man wants companionship as well. Sex alone will not truly bring about the man you would want. But women are taught to advertise that first and foremost. There is nothing wrong with a woman being sexy and expressing her sexuality. However, an inordinate amount of anything can be self destructive. The misuse of sex brings about a harsh side of women that produces the mentality of a whore. Since women realize that men want sex and many men want sex for nothing they resort to expecting some form of compensation. This in the process makes our relationships deteriorate. Love has become a false hope while sex is a medium of exchange for some type of profit.

The Pimp/Whore game is destroying the Black family as well as the Black community. Love is something that has to be seriously and sincerely worked for. We have to establish relationships that are healthy through co-operation. You already know when you enter into a relationship what you want from that particular relationship. The question you must ask yourself is if this person is willing to provide the things you want. Then you must ask yourself if this person is willing and capable of giving you what you want. Then you must ask yourself and the other person involved what they want and expect in this relationship. After all of that, you then must ask yourself if you are willing to give those things to that person. When I speak of wants and needs this applies to the mental, spiritual, physical and emotional concerns of a person.

This corrupt world that we live in has caused us to be shaped into inequity. We are brought up nowadays to lie to get what we want. We are being raised to deceive people when we are not willing to give something of ourselves. The subtle images of your mother making you tell the bill collector that she is not home when you know that she is. We as human beings follow people by example. One thing might come out of their mouth but we pay more attention to what they are doing. Do as I say and not as I do have become the norm. So we grow up with the same mentality when we become involved in an intimate relationship. We lie to get what we want then turn around and deceive a person so we don't have to give them what they want. We all are guilty of it at some point in our life. This chapter is for us to be more cognizant of this behavior and work towards removing it from our life. A man and a woman are two halves of one being and the highest level of love is manifested when they come together through work and commitment towards that goal. Having the right motive and establishing the right foundation can create heaven on earth for two people that are in love. But if we decide to deceive and mislead we can continue to bring about the hell that many relationships suffer. Let us first try to be honest with ourselves then with each other and then we can stop acting like pimps and whores.

3
ESTABLISHING RELATIONSHIPS

Intertwining thoughts that complement our soul
PaPa Sak

It seems simple but appears to be difficult nowadays for men and women to establish relationships. We meet each other based upon physical attraction and usually build on that alone. Physical attraction is based upon preference but relationships are established. How relationships are established you might ask? It comes down to the two people involved in this relationship naturally. From an even deeper aspect we must first deal with how the two people perceive one another. If the perception is wrong or tainted it may decide how they treat one another.

I once had an associate that at one particular time I considered a friend. He and I hung around similar circles and shared similar view points. One day in particular we were talking about music. I wanted us to work on a project together doing music. We had worked together before and everything went smooth so I suggested we work together again. During our conversation he happened to mention to me that he went to a business seminar the weekend prior to us meeting. He explained that the keynote speaker explained that there are three types of people you deal with in business. One was called the blue people, the other was called the green people and the third was called the red people.

The blue people were the people that looked up to you. They admired you as a person and they were what you called a subordinate. These blue people could be people you supervise, they could be children or they could be people that come to you for advice. Through labor, age, rank or authority you definitely hold a higher position than they do.

He went on to explain that the green people were considered your equals. These were the people that dealt with you on your level. They may even be more critical of you because they are your peer. For the most part they are equally dependant on the relationship as you are. You don't have to answer to them and they don't have to answer to you. In the workplace or elsewhere you basically hold the same rank.

Then you have what is known as the red people. These are the people that you look up to. They more than likely hold rank over you in some way or another. They could be your supervisor, a judge, hold rank over you in some military sense. They could be your parents or an elder. The bottom line is that you are subordinate to these people.

I asked him a question after he explained the different types of people. I wondered if we were over critical of each other because we were peers. He looked me dead in the eye and replied. 'That's your problem; you need to look at me as one of the red people'. Needless to say we are no longer friends.

Part of establishing relationships is grasping how a person perceives you. You cannot always make the right judgment call because so many people put up a façade. However there is one thing that can help you understand how they perceive you. You can pay attention to how they treat you. Are they considerate of your needs and wants? Are they attentive to your concerns? When they speak to you is it in an authoritative tone or is the tone friendly. Of course men and women start relationships off like this in the beginning stages. They may even pretend to be nice just to get what they want in the relationship. The one thing you should consider is that a person can't hide being themselves for too long. The more time you spend with them the more you see them for who they are. Eventually they will show you how they perceive you. You must pay attention to those signs. The first time they decide to yell at you or be verbally abusive you have to put your foot down. Regardless to how much you like them you must demand that it never happens again. You could end the relationship there or you can give them another chance but you make sure they know not to cross that line.

Many choose to argue back. I am guilty of arguing back but what you eventually produce is a relationship that has two co-dependents of an abusive relationship.

What I would suggest is that you write down or openly verbalize what you will accept and not accept in an intimate relationship. It is always best to do this before sexual intercourse. Sex always clouds the mind; especially when it is good sex. Two adults can have a civilized conversation without beating each other down with words. Physical abuse is totally out of the question regardless if it is male or female that is doing the abusing. True love is an enduring thing and is way beyond the shallow realm of physical features. The best way to endure is to establish a certain way you expect to be treated. When you explain this to people they believe that it takes away from the romance. Constant break-ups and bitter divorces is what truly takes away from romance. It makes both men and women put up guards that hinder them from growing with a soul mate. Soul mates are not ready made; they are developed into that through time, patients, compatibility and love. Intimate relationships will not last without a foundation. People will organize and carefully select shoes better than they organize relationships and select mates. This concept of thinking is what has brought about so many broken families and broken homes.

We might tend to blame the other party in a relationship for mistreating us. The fact of the matter is that many times we allow ourselves to be mistreated by being complacent. Because we believe we are in love we allow things to slide that eventually grow into a cancer. This cancer then causes a rift in the relationship that cannot be repaired. Learn to establish relationships before intimacy and you will definitely sift through a lot of bullshit that comes your way. You tried and failed the other way now try it a new way and see your results. You will soon see who really has your best interest in mind or who just wants to use you for their own wants without willingness to give you what you need and want in return.

4
YOU GET WHAT YOU ARE!

Deception is my weapon even against my self
PaPa Sak

Who are you? Answer that question without giving your name, race, religion, nationality or political affiliation. Can you accurately describe who you are from a spiritual, mental and behavioral description? Regardless of your religious beliefs are you truly at peace spiritually with how you live? I can honestly say I am not. Yet I am striving to reach that level of mastery. Are you owning up to the sins you are bringing into your own life? Are you checking the corrupt thoughts that might flow through your head? Are you paying attention to the way you act and treat others? We all believe consciously or unconsciously that we are the center of attention. We naturally think of our own personal needs and wants first. Do you however, think of your friends, family and peers with good intentions? I'm asking these questions for you to consider the energy that you are sending out into the world. They are like waves or vibrations that eventually return to their source. You are basically sending out what you will eventually receive in return.

Did you know that anything that is weak or lacks the proper amount of strength is devil? We talk about the devil being a liar. We talk about the devil deceiving us. But ask yourself honestly, if the devil was coming from a position of strength and power why would he have to lie to you? If he was confident about his position in the world why would he have to trick you in order to convince you to take his side? If he was coming from a position of real strength he would show you how he got his strength and the evidence would prove his case to be true. But if he has something to hide he will not show you that because it will sway you the other way. That in turn is what we do to ourselves and to each other. We lie to ourselves about what we want and what we need. We lie to others about what we are willing to do and what we are not willing to do for them. Sometimes we are so weak for another person we compromise who and what we are to keep that person around. That is the real concept of worshiping false and idol gods. So we allow people to take advantage of us because we are too weak to stand up for ourselves.

It may not be a physical weakness; it could be an emotional, spiritual or mental weakness that allows you to be misused. Sex without an established relationship can bring about emotional weakness. You can be so emotionally attached to the person that you can't break away from something you know is unhealthy for you. You can be easily influenced to do wrong because your peers have chose to do wrong. This is a clear sign of a mental weakness. Spiritual weakness can manifest in you not treating yourself properly. You begin to believe you are not worthy of what is due to every human being. Your mouth might say it but your actions display something entirely different.

Case and point; you are a woman that is dating a guy that wants to see you every day in the beginning. After awhile he starts gradually slowing it down for some reason or another. Now when you call him he doesn't answer the phone as often as he once did. You get an excuse here and a reason there. He calls you on his terms and you roll with the change of routine. But now your intuition is telling you something isn't right. You are getting a certain feeling or vibe that suggests that he is not being totally honest with you. You still let things continue because after all you don't have any proof. So as time progresses you begin to see that you are losing any form of control into how this relationship is going. Yet you both are in the relationship it appears that it is strictly on his terms. Every time you speak your mind it starts an argument. At this point he might threaten to end the relationship because you are adding to his problems. After all, you don't have any proof that he is doing anything wrong. So you let this continue until eventually your relationship has deteriorated to the point of no repair. Then when it is all said and done; you ask what happened and now you are spiritually drained.

I'll tell you what happened. You became complacent with the fantasy of being in love. At some point you were more in love with being in love than you were with your mate. He on the other hand got what he wanted and is no longer as hungry for what you provided for him initially. In fact, he doesn't have to have what you provided anymore. It might still bring him pleasure, like sex for instance. But it has less value to him now so you let him establish a new course of action. When the rules changed you should have changed but instead you allowed him to continue to manipulate the relationship. You are so dumbfounded that you just want to do whatever it takes to make the relationship work. He knows this; so the threat of a break-up makes you weaken in your position. Your intuition is ringing a loud alarm but since you can't prove that there is wrong doing you silence your spiritual alarm. Suppressing this spiritual warning makes your spirit lose the eagerness to do what it was created to do. Since you are in a pattern of suppressing your intuition it begins to malfunction because it is clouded by your false hopes of true love. When in fact you had forfeited true love the moment you allowed him to take total control of the reigns in your relationship. Then one day you find out that he was being untrue and you look at him as a dirty dog. He dogged you so bad that your heart is broken into a million pieces. Yet you still refuse to acknowledge the dog in yourself that allowed you to attract another dog. You were weak to what could have been, by suppressing your spirit when it was warning you to what was really going on. You attracted what you are.

Have you noticed that dogs live off of feeding their appetites? When humans live strictly off of their appetites their spiritual and mental capacities become inactive. Living for your appetites weakens your own power and makes you a slave to your physical wants. Most of us are guilty of it. That is when a woman may be with a man that is a dog when it comes to sex. She may be a dog when it comes to worshipping a façade. Her lust for some ideal makes her appetite grow to the point where it misleads her into hoping for something that is not there. Remember men depend on logic while women depend on intuition. Both male and female have both faculties but one gender leans towards the other more naturally. Logic is based upon what we know while intuition is based upon what we feel. If you do not heed the spiritual and mental insight that we all possess you are functioning on the level of an animal. So don't expect to attract anything other than that.

Acknowledge your weaknesses so that you can work towards removing them in your life. Men and women are two halves of one being. When we come together we can bring the best or the worst out of each other depending on our weaknesses. If we pay attention to our own and help our mate pay attention to his or her own we can work towards removing them from our lives. That is the objective of people that seek a higher love.

5
NIGGAS

Decimating the future with my dick generation after generation
PaPa Sak

This is a word today that many people refuse to use. In fact, the word nigga is nowadays referred to as the N-word. It is ridiculous for people to make this word such a taboo. The truth is that we as Black people who are the descendants of slaves have many characteristics of the derogatory word Nigga. We act on our appetites. The White man in fact was the first to show us how to connive and manipulate based upon our appetites. So we are only acting like our oppressors. Please forgive me if you think that I went on a geo-political tirade.

My purpose for bringing this subject up is to point out the fact we were taught to be this way. We were conditioned as a people to be irresponsible, lack commitment and shun obligation. We were also taught through example how to not take responsibility for the wrongs we do. Slavery was such a traumatic experience for our ancestors it would be silly not to believe that it made some of them mentally ill. Not to mention the spiritual, emotional and physical ramifications of such brutal treatment. So imagine millions of people that believe they are sane but are not who have not been treated for this post traumatic stress. Then they produce children that suffer the same sicknesses without any treatment. In the process of this inner turmoil it grows but no one seems to notice because many people in the same community suffer the same problems. Then finally a generation comes about that seeks civil rights and integration. While they fight for a good cause they have yet to address the fundamental problems in their everyday life. They choose to seek material goals instead of healthy resolutions to solve the emotional, mental and spiritual diseases that plague their lives. This is the reality of the Black man and woman of America who are descendants of slaves. We still have a lot of nigga in us. So it is necessary that we address the pandemic before it is too late. This chapter will be about those characteristics. Let us humbly look in the mirror before we put this tag on someone else.

A nigga doesn't want to worry about responsibility. When he deals with commitment he deals with it on his terms and his terms alone. He will pretend he wants commitment for sex but a nigga really doesn't. A nigga that is of legal age to be considered an adult believes that he is grown so he doesn't have to answer to anyone. Except of course to the person that is paying him he doesn't have to submit to anyone or their rules. Even if he agrees with the rules he still doesn't have to abide them. He will say things like 'I'm grown I don't have to answer to anyone'. But if you committed yourself to those rules he will expect you to live up to them nevertheless. It might be okay for him to go out and cheat but he better not find out that you are doing the same. The shiftless lazy nigga is not as relevant today as it once was. In modern post millennium America, most niggas are willing to get money because they know it gives them the upper hand in this society. The modern shiftless nigga may have nice cars, even a nice home, but he will not have a healthy monogamous relationship. He may have a few women that he has sex with. He strings these women along giving them the idea that he might settle down with them. He probably won't because he is comfortable with not answering to anyone but still being able to have the pleasure of sex. Many women don't put their foot down because they are hoping he chooses them. But think about it, how can he really respect you when you are settling for something that is less than you? With sex many women give a Nigga more power than he can handle.

Now we are in the generation of 'Baby Mamas'; not wives. We are in the generation where sex without obligation is just getting your swerve on. It is normal to have sex before marriage today. I'm not a religious nut first and foremost. I also have my sins to face. But let us tell the truth for a change. Having sex before marriage doesn't obligate anyone. It gives both parties involved the freedom to do as they please. That is why God or whatever being you give praise to forbids sex before marriage. Most of us are guilty of it. Niggas in fact live off your weakness to sex so he doesn't have to commit. That is why the word bitch comes out his mouth so quickly. He knows that you are acting like a dog that is in heat that happens to be a female. But who cares; you get to bust a nut and he gets to bust a nut.

Now children are born under these conditions. They are the product of broken relationships, broken families and lack of commitments. So what do you do, you raise your boys to go out and do the same thing to other women that was done to you. I've known mothers who think that it is cute and will welcome their sons home when he doesn't want to commit to a woman he has started a family with. We encourage boys to be niggas by not teaching them how to be responsible with sex. Whatever freedom you believe you have; you must consider that freedom comes with responsibility. Everything in the universe requires certain rules. You cannot name anything that is in this universe that doesn't have principles or rules and regulations. That's like trying to bounce a rock like a basketball. That's like using your feet to eat. If you want the best results you must follow the rules. However, we are in a world that tells us to break the rules if we can get away with it. I've been a rebel my entire life and I know what rules to break and which ones not to break. Because of bad habits I have broken rules I know I shouldn't break and really couldn't complain when I got negative results. A Nigga will want freedom but will not want the responsibility that comes with such freedom.

Now that you have an idea of how a nigga can act. The question you must ask yourself; is if you are willing to sift through the niggas and find a man that wants to commit to you. First and foremost don't give him what he wants without him giving you what you want. From a metaphysical standpoint; don't allow his energy to penetrate your energy without him proving himself willing and able to take care of your needs. Niggas will run from any sign that indicates that they have to make a commitment. You will narrow down the bullshit. Niggas only love on a physical or carnal level. They love you based upon what you can do for them. That is naturally that pimp mentality. During the reconstruction period when the civil war was over many blacks didn't have a way to make a living. What many men decided to do was have their women go back to the old slave master and ask for food, goods and money in return for sexual favors. Since the slave master was sneaking down to the slave quarters to take the sex during slavery the male slave grew accustomed to sharing his woman. Now that they were hungry and homeless they picked up the same patterns after slavery. Niggas have learned to detach themselves from their women while still getting the pleasure of sex. Niggas have also learned not to take responsibility for their actions. NIGGAS ARE AFRAID OF REVOLUTION. Revolution means change. I once heard an intelligent pro black militant brother say that the only thing better than pussy is new pussy. A nigga comes in many different angles. They are activists, poets, athletes, police officers, doctors, lawyers, actors and even preachers.

Let us deal with the word and meaning of Nigga properly. Let's go to the root of the cause that makes us act like these characteristics then work to change them.

6
BITCHES

There is a difference in being strong and being mean!
PaPa Sak

This is a difficult subject to address. The word bitch is such a taboo when a woman is called that nowadays. Unless of course women are calling each other that it is considered a vicious name. On the street it is part of the norm to call a woman a bitch. I address that in my book 'The Street Code'. In this chapter for this book I once again want to deal with how a woman acts that makes this word so relevant.

First and foremost womanhood is taught not naturally grown into. Just like manhood it holds a certain criteria. Someone of the female gender must consider what makes her a woman besides the legal age of an adult. She also has to consider that a career doesn't define womanhood either. In ancient Kemit (Egypt) there were gods and goddesses that ruled and were honored. It wasn't a patriarchal or matriarchal order but in fact both sexes participated as rulers. I'm saying this to point out that both man and woman have the ability to rise to the level of mastery. Every person has the ability to be their worse or their best. Human beings are social beings so there is no doubt we can be influenced either way. What you might want to pay attention to is which way are you being persuaded. I will point out symptoms for you to recognize if you are defining the word bitch.

When you look at it for what it is, this is describing a female that doesn't want to be right. It is some scandalous females in the world that will get you caught up. Some females will set you up to be robbed and killed. Some will offer you sex so that you can get killed by one of their homeboys. A bitch will be your girlfriend then go and fuck your homeboy behind your back. A bitch will try to do something to hurt you because you don't want to be with her anymore. If she is your lady and she sees that you are being successful she will try to ruin it for you. A bitch's logic is that if he makes it big he might trade me in. She lets her insecurities make decisions for her. Her emotions have more control over her than her mind.

A bitch will be fucking two or three different niggas and accuse the one she likes the most of being her baby's father. Even though she is probably not sure who the father is she will still accuse whomever she wants. She will get an abortion behind your back if she knows you want the baby and she doesn't. She is not even woman enough to tell you to your face before she gets the abortion. A bitch will fuck her home girl's man because she is jealous of what she has. A bitch will cheat on her husband or boyfriend just because he made her mad. Then at the right time she will admit it, just to hurt you. A bitch is easy to fuck but hard to live with. She may look good but she doesn't act good. A bitch is conceited and acts as if she is better than people because of her looks. Sometimes it's the other way around; a bitch can act polite and respectful in public but be a demon seed behind closed doors.

A bitch thinks that every man that is polite to her is trying to get with her. A bitch will use her children to hurt her baby's daddy. She will even turn her children against him because he doesn't want to be with her anymore. A bitch will try to turn homeboys against each other. She will really try to break up friendships if she has fucked around with either homeboys one time or another. A bitch will hide birth control pills behind her husband's back or get her tubes tied behind his back. A bitch will hit you in your face and when you hit her back she calls the police on you. When the police come to your house she plays the victim as if she didn't do anything wrong and will allow you to go to jail even though she was the violent one. A bitch will teach her daughter not to trust a man because *she* didn't choose the right one. A bitch is only out for herself even when she is in a relationship. A bitch doesn't know the difference from being strong and being mean. A bitch thinks all men will cheat so she uses this belief to do her dirt.

I could go on for thousands of pages but I think you get the idea. Now if you are a female and you have found yourself doing any of these things, at that particular time you were acting like a **BITCH**. Many women have a little bitch in them and many women have a lot of bitch in them. I must admit when I was writing this part a few faces came to mind. **If** you want to stop being a bitch or rid yourself of a few characteristics you should take heed to the symptoms and see how they apply to you.

7
THE ABILITY TO RESPOND

The definition of manhood is commitment, obligation,
responsibility and observance of the laws that govern the universe.
PaPa Sak

If you really pay attention to the word responsibility it is in fact a compound word. Those two words that have come together are ability and response. A man understands that he has to have the ability to respond to the wants and needs of his family. A man understands that he has to have the ability to respond to the needs of his community. Not just on a local scale but also on a global scale. Of course many men are not capable of having the influence to address the needs of the entire planet. This concept of thinking that I refer to is more of playing your role as a member of this global society. Every man was born and permitted to exist for some purpose or objective. It is his duty to fulfill that purpose. Manhood is much more complicated than reaching a certain age. There are particulars that we as men have to fulfill that determine if we are men or not. Many of us believe that money determines if we are men but this is not true. Money is only a tool that is used to fulfill our duty and obligation.

As far as family is concerned a man must take care of the needs and wants of his family. The wants of his family are really just a bonus to his responsibilities. In truth his duty is to take care of the needs of his family. If he is married or engaged he has obligations to his wife or fiancé. If he has vowed to stay faithful then he must uphold that obligation. He gave his word before the Supreme Being that he would be loyal to that particular woman. If he is permitted to have more than one wife in his religious beliefs than he must commit to however many wives he has. A man that doesn't honor his commitment to his wife is not living up to the responsibilities of a man. If she forfeits his obligation through divorce than he is no longer obligated. Some men have committed adultery in a moment of weakness. That doesn't necessarily make them less of a man but it does point out that they are not living up to the criteria of a man. They have fallen short. Being a man is a practical thing. It is more or less what you practice daily. Making a mistake doesn't make you less than a man but the consistency of making mistakes makes you less than a man. That is when a male practices shunning his duty.

A man that has children must have the ability to respond to the needs of his offspring. He may have the obstacles of baby mamas, ex-wives or ex-one-night stands. This still should not deter him from his duty as a father. A real man will leap over those hurdles to take care of his responsibility. Many males will father children and leave it up to the woman to do all of the upbringing. If he is in a position where he doesn't have much money he will use this as an excuse to not be a father. Some males will provide financial help to their child through child support but this still doesn't make you a man. What makes you a man is your participation in the child's upbringing. A child needs support, guidance, discipline, education and love. Both parents are responsible for providing such things. When one of the parents neglects these needs the child suffers in so many ways. A man uses practical methods to provide what is needed for his family. If you are doing anything other than that you are less than a man.

Lastly a man has an obligation to his self and his community. Many young men are brought up without fathers so they have to figure out what a man is as legal adults. Every man has a talent or a gift that purpose has granted him. It is his obligation to use that talent to advance the plight of humanity. That is the true understanding of charity. You are supposed to give not only money but resources to those in need. This is what separates us from the rest of the animal kingdom. The male influence has not been present in raising many boys in the Black community. This imbalance of nature is causing the break-up of families. It creates a void in which many boys never grow up to be men. They shun their responsibility because they haven't been properly taught on what responsibility entails. So they never grasp the concept of responsibility when it comes to family, community and to self. We have many black males roaming around aimlessly without fulfilling their purpose. Your talent and your gifts is also your duty to share it with the world. Anything less than that is the practice of being less than a man.

8
THE INTUITIVE SPIRIT

The feminine side of the duality in God
PaPa Sak

Womanhood is an experience that as a man I am not that arrogant to suggest I understand. However, I will go as far as to say that I have somewhat of an understanding when it comes to the nature of things. In chapter six I dealt with the negative things that a woman can do. I have met queens in my day that will shame the word bitch from any man's vocabulary. They have their flaws but are beautiful in every sense of the word. I love them; past and present. These women rise above their emotions into the thinking of goddesses. They deal with a more spiritual aspect of womanhood. They have an intimate connection with intuition.

The intuitive woman allows the divinity within herself to guide her movements. She may not have mastered her intuition but she is seeking the methods to do so. Her beauty is beyond the physical realm even though she may be physically attractive. Women in general rely on their intuition more frequently than men. Many men rely on logic but that is based upon what we know. Since we are still babies in knowledge our logic can only take us so far. There is a macrocosm of spirit that our individual microcosm spirit is connected to. Tapping into that infinite power opens your heart and mind to an entirely different realm of thinking. It broadens your horizon to see things from a spiritual center referred to as your third eye. A woman that rises above her emotions has better insight because of this.

An intuitive woman will not ignore the warning signs when she is in an unhealthy relationship. She will be informed by her inner spirit of the impending danger. She can speak her mind and communicate properly listening to her spirit and not her emotion. You might ask how a woman can listen to her spirit instead of her emotions. How can she tell the difference? She can tell by her level of peace. If she is guided by anger than her emotions will get the best of her. This is not to suggest that a woman shouldn't become angry. I am making the point that the only proper way for her to handle a problem is to calm her anger before approaching the issue. Naturally a man should do the same. However, the nature of a man and woman differ in many ways. I've seen women put men in check with kind words but firm resilience. An emotional woman will lock horns with a man accomplishing nothing but an argument. An intuitive woman will make him understand his wrongs by intuitively knowing how to deliver them. An intuitive woman will leave her man if he doesn't want to correct his wrongs. An emotional woman will want to beat him down with his wrongs until he submits. Which more than likely he will never do and even if he does she will not want him any longer. An intuitive woman recognizes the power of being a woman and doesn't try to be a man. The emotional woman will say 'What is good for the goose is good for the gander'. This is not the ways of the intuitive woman because she doesn't have to submit to any man. She has the power to make sound decisions for a sound future for herself. How can an intuitive woman submit to a man? She should never submit to a man but she should submit to the god in man. If he is not submitting to a higher being that makes him accountable for his actions than she shouldn't be bothered. The intuitive woman is sublime and her beauty is supreme.

Men and women are different and not just physiologically. Life is formed in the womb of woman. She is the incubator to life in all its abundance. She receives what the man has given her and she produces an end result. The man puts the vision in motion but the woman materializes that vision. The feminine side of the duality in god goes way beyond giving birth. Look at the planet earth for instance. It rotates 1037 1/3 miles per hour in empty space. It produces and sustains millions and trillions of life forms every day. She takes the energy that the sun gives her and produces the wonderful things we call nature. That is womanhood. She sustains what she has produced and understands her obligation. That is why she is called mother earth. Now the flip side of that is something to also consider. The earth has cycles that are known to us as winter, spring, summer and autumn. Though the earth has these cycles she rises above these different climates (emotions) to still provide us with nature's wonders. An intuitive woman will understand to do the same. If she interacts with a man that cannot value her intuitive power; that very same intuition will direct her to leave him alone. And she will listen.

Prayer or meditative thought are the methods to tapping into this power. I have heard many women ask me questions about their relationships. I will listen and I will always use the phrase 'one plus one is two'. That means if it doesn't add up then something is wrong. These women in *every* instance knew that there was a problem. But for some reason they felt like they needed to hear it from an outside source. Their intuition was ringing loudly trying to warn them of something they may not have had proof but actions of the male counterpart didn't add up. Don't listen to what a man says but what he does and that includes me as well. A man will let you know in many ways that he doesn't want you. Your intuition will let you know; you just have to pay attention. A man will let you know that all he wants to do is hit that ass and nothing more. Your intuition will point out his actions. A man will let you know that he is dragging you along in an aimless relationship until he finds something else or something he thinks is better. Your intuition will give you the signs of his actions. That is the purpose of spirituality not religion. Spirituality protects you from things if you listen. It is something that women naturally inherit but choose to silence because many are controlled by their emotions.

Lastly, a man protects the woman from the outside world. This is a harsh and cruel world and the woman should be protected from all its brutalities. On the other hand, the woman protects a man from himself. The bible refers to the rib taken from Adam to create Eve but it is a much deeper understanding to this story. The rib protects vital organs in the human body. The liver, the kidney and other important parts are protected by your rib cage. From a spiritual standpoint that is how a woman protects a man from himself. Through her intuition she protects him from danger that his logic cannot foresee.

9
FAIL TO PLAN, PLAN TO FAIL

For attention you chose sex for love I chose lust
We both got to climax but couldn't build too much
PaPa Sak

I will not be long with this chapter because it is self explanatory. A relationship has certain building blocks that are necessary for it to endure. You can love someone and not be 'in love' with someone. There are three main levels of love. Those three levels of love are physical, mental and spiritual. For a relationship to truly last it has to be more than just physical and mental. A truly spiritual relationship will not fall apart. The only way this could happen is if one or both parties abandon the spiritual connection. I will touch on each level of love briefly then explain the planning aspect of a relationship.

The physical aspect dwells on how a person looks. How a person makes you feel when you are having sex with them. How you make them feel when you are having sex with them. Many men judge women by beauty. On the other hand, many women judge men by image. People will assume I mean the same thing when I say image and beauty. They have different perspectives when it comes to love and relationships. A man will think of her beauty and how she can pleasure him first. Sex will be the initial motivator that determines if he will approach. I'm not saying that women do not pay attention to these things. Right now I'm dealing with the man. His choice depends on what he is physically attracted to for sexual reasons. If he is an enlightened man he will eventually strive for something more than just her physical qualifications. On a physical level she has to be sexually appealing for her to become a candidate for courtship or relationship.

Women dealing with men on a physical level can be slightly complicated. A woman can openly date a man that she is not physically attracted to and sincerely fall for him. Not because she is less shallow than a man but because he provides something else that satisfies her wants. For instance, a woman will date a man that is old and decrepit if he is financially secure. She may find that his security is more important than his looks. It is still on a physical level but the physical involves money and resources. A woman will consider how she looks dating this man and can make sense of the situation by pointing out he has money. Her image is secure. A woman can date a tough guy that everyone is afraid of because she feels secure. She may not be sexually attracted to him but the image of respect and security might make him sexy to her. She could like him because of his style or his flavor, etc. I'm pointing all of this out so both men and women can understand what is most important to them. You cannot plan properly if you don't know what you want the most. Go after what you want on a physical level so you can build on the mental and spiritual level.

When you love someone on a mental level they have attracted you by their ways and actions. You have a fundamental connection of who this person really is. You might appreciate her or his political viewpoints or their spiritual opinions. You might like the way he or she sings, raps, dances or talks. You appreciate the way this person thinks. You value his or her contributions to the world. This is a beautiful way to build a relationship because you can both strive for an ideal. Working together for a common cause strengthens any bond especially when the people involved are successful.

The spiritual level of love has a long lasting effect. Some may believe that I mean religion. Spirituality surpasses any religious dogma or belief. I'm not suggesting that you abandon your beliefs; I am merely suggesting that you pay more attention to spiritual issues more than religious ones. Religious issues dwell upon if you believe in Jesus, Muhammad or Moses, etc. Spiritual issues dwell upon if you are at peace with whatever God you serve. It deals more with being at peace with yourself. Spirituality addresses how you apply scripture to your life to make it better. It deals with fundamental concerns on applying solutions to your problems. Spirituality points out road maps to get to heaven on earth. 'Thy kingdom come, thy will be done, on earth as it is in heaven'. You are surrounding yourself with peace by following the principles that govern the universe. When you are spiritually in love, both you and your mate have that connection. You are divinely guided and can create heaven on earth.

When you plan to get into an intimate relationship with someone you have to cover all basics. You must understand your mate's physical needs and wants. You must understand your mate's mental needs and wants. But before you do that you must first know your own. Then sit down and map out a future with one another based upon the needs and wants of both people involved. The next step is to discover what each other are willing to compromise and what you are not willing to compromise. Once you make those plans then and only then can you take your relationship to another level. People fall in love every day in a physical and mental way. But they don't secure that love because they don't plan how to make it work. As the relationship progresses or degenerates you begin to discover things about your mate that you might dislike. If you are more prepared and well planned you can work through the kinks in armor. Love can be very fickle if you don't have a mutual plan that strengthens your bond. That is a relationship worth fighting for.

10
GOD IS LOVE

Imprinted in the sky and tasted by God
PaPa Sak

We are in the image and likeness of God. No matter what you call him you have to bear witness that there is a greater force that exists besides you as a person. If you were to include the collective bodies of humanity you will admit that your will cannot stand up against the totality of humanity. This is not a chapter dealing with how you perceive God. It is a chapter that identifies the God that is in you. The human anatomy is the perfected vessel that is used for the ultimate expression of God. In the English language the word 'is' can be recognized as an equal sign in mathematics. So when we say that 'God is Love' we are pointing out that Love is the Creator. We are also suggesting that love is the most creative force in the universe.

Love being the most creative force suggests that there are infinite possibilities to love. Two people that are truly 'in love' have the ability to reach the stars. Since man and woman are two halves of one being we are a power house when we co-operate. The battle of the sexes has hindered our development because we have not been right by ourselves and one another. That is why I had to address the problems first in this book. We are basically digging ourselves out of a hole. Because we do not know how to treat one another so we become victims of our own corruption. We become weaklings mentally, spiritually and emotionally so we allow ourselves to be mistreated. Love removes the insecurities that doubt has bestowed upon us. It allows us the ability to trust. We don't trust in a naïve way but in a divine way. This helps us see through the drama that someone is willing to inflict on us. Love is the pathway to heaven on earth. It is the pinnacle of success; no matter what kind of treasures you possess they mean nothing without a life of love.

If you believe in God or not you must at least believe in the divinity of humanity. The side of humanity that wants to be right by people does exist. We have to reach into our heart and find love for ourselves first. Build that to the point where we know how to treat ourselves properly on all levels of mind, body and spirit. Though we are striving the process of applying these things can be a life long journey. When you find someone to love who loves you just the same you can build up that union to the point of divine power and beauty. Every human should experience this joy. The world would be a much better place if we all did. That is the concept and idea of 'God is love'. It is the ideal in us all. It is the most creative force in the universe. Imagine the possibilities.

11
THE ULTIMATE GOAL

There is a prerequisite behavior for entering into heaven or hell!
PaPa Sak

The ultimate goal is heaven on earth. When we develop ourselves to the level of love we can create heaven in our environment. First we create love for ourselves without inordinate selfishness. Then we create love for each other in the same process. Then we create heaven in our community and after that we spread it throughout the world. It might seem farfetched because we have yet to establish love amongst ourselves. Love for self and your mate is the foundation for family and then community. We can become the beacon light of the world if we address our problems and rectify them. Thy Kingdom come, Thy will be done, on earth as it is in heaven.

Also from PaPa Sak on Amazon &
www.ensbooks.com

Coming soon from PaPa Sak on Amazon &
www.ensbooks.com

PaPa Sak is a voice for the streets and the Black community for those that are usually misrepresented and misunderstood. His goal is to bring humanity to these characters and to bring understanding to other unpopular perspectives. His characters come from people he has known or interacted with at one time or another. One of his main focuses is to shed spiritual insight on stories that should be told in the Black experience and abroad. He is also a profound orator and inspirational speaker ranging in spoken word poetry, gang & street lifestyle, male and female relationships, manhood training, spirituality, Hip Hop and history. He is a literary force in the new Millennium. You can also find him on Facebook as

Novelist PaPa Sak, Twitter as PaPaSak71
and www.ensbooks.com